A McDADE NOVEL

FORBIDDEN WANT

SCARLETT FINN

<u>Also by Scarlett Finn</u>

GO NOVELS
GO WITH IT
GO IT ALONE
GO ALL OUT
GO ALL IN
GO FULL CIRCLE

EXILE
HIDE & SEEK
KISS CHASE

WRECK & RUIN
RUIN ME
RUIN HIM

**THE BRANDED
SERIES**
BRANDED
SCARRED
MARKED

**FORBIDDEN
PREQUEL DUET**
ALL. ONLY.
ONLY YOURS

TO DIE FOR...
TO DIE FOR TRUTH
TO DIE FOR HONOR
TO DIE FOR VIRTUE
TO DIE FOR DUTY
TO DIE FOR LOVE

**LOVE AGAINST THE ODDS
STANDALONE COLLECTION**
SWEET SEAS
HEIR'S AFFAIR
RESCUED
MAESTRO'S MUSE
GETTING TRICKY
THIRTEEN
REMEMBER WHEN...
RELUCTANT SUSPICION
XY FACTOR

NOTHING TO...
NOTHING TO HIDE
NOTHING TO LOSE
NOTHING TO DECLARE
NOTHING TO US
NOTHING TO SAY
NOTHING TO GAIN
NOTHING TO YOU
NOTHING TO THIS

THE FORBIDDEN NOVELS
FORBIDDEN DESIRE
FORBIDDEN WANT
FORBIDDEN WISH
FORBIDDEN NEED

KINDRED SERIES
RAVEN
SWALLOW
CUCKOO
SWIFT
FALCON
FINCH

THE EXPLICIT SERIES
EXPLICIT INSTRUCTION
EXPLICIT DETAIL
EXPLICIT MEMORY

MISTAKE DUET
MISTAKE ME NOT
SLEIGHT MISTAKE

**RISQUÉ & HARROW
INTERTWINED**
TAKE A RISK
FIGHTING FATE
RISK IT ALL
FIGHTING BACK
GAME OF RISK

LOST & FOUND
LOST
FOUND

ONE

POUNCING ONTO HER elbows, Sersha awoke suddenly.

Bed low to the floor, black satin sheets, stag heads embroidered in the corner of the pillowcases. Stag. Ire McDade's nightclub. His private bedroom. Their deal. Sex for silence.

Except she was alone.

"McDade," she whispered, touching her lips.

What happened? She'd done as told, stripped off and slipped into his bed, then waited and waited… Apparently, he'd never arrived.

Casting the sheet aside, she got up to check the closet. No one. Her hand brushed along the hanging clothes until she snagged a shirt to button it over her bare body.

In the bathroom… Still no one. And no steam or water droplets to suggest recent use.

Leaving by the second door, she rounded into the long living space. A large segmented semi-circular window at the other end let in daylight.

Passing between the seating area and stocked bar, she skirted the dining table to peek outside. No one was out there either. The kitchen by the window tempted her closer. Drinks in the fridge, coffee, nothing to eat. Padded stools, better suited for a bar than a kitchen island, suggested they used the space for entertaining rather than as a full-time residence.

What kind of home would a man like Ire McDade live in?

And where had he gone? Last night she'd assumed he would come to her in bed and hadn't asked for further instructions. Whatever he expected, he hadn't been explicit, and there was no way she'd hang around all day waiting and wondering.

Real or not, she took a shower and put her dress back on, pairing it with one of Ire's suit jackets. For warmth. And to hide the morning-after shame. Not that there had been a night-before. Wasn't sex what he wanted? Why demand complete sexual submission only to pass up the chance to exploit it?

He didn't seem like the type to flake on someone. Or the type to sleep next to a sexually accessible woman and keep his hands off. Unless he'd changed his mind about their deal. Shit. What would that mean for their sex tape? Could it already be out there?

Dread became more real in the vacant office. From the internal windows there, she checked out the club below. Empty too.

Being alone was eerie. Everything looked different bathed in the sun streaming through the glazed roof panels. She hadn't even known they existed. With the club lights and the night always above, she'd never given the ceiling much thought.

The office wasn't locked. Good. At least she wasn't a prisoner. No one stood on the stairs, or even at the bottom of them. Where was security? Off-duty? Had she slept through the apocalypse?

The club entrance was closed. No big deal, except how did she open such massive doors? They folded back, maybe, hinges in the middle—a smaller section opened in from the outside before she got that far. What the hell? Another thing she'd never noticed. A door within a door.

Stepping outside, past the guy who'd opened the door, her focus stuck on her McDade protector, Daly, waiting by the Bentley at the curb.

"Going to work?" he asked, opening the back door.

"Home first," she said, frowning when he held the takeout coffee cup toward her. "What is that?"

"Venti hazelnut latte, skinny, extra shot."

She laughed, taking the cup from him to sniff the steam. "How do you know my coffee?"

"Normal day is breaking kneecaps and noses collecting cash," he said. "Getting a guy to spill on your coffee order is cake."

Uh… "Okay."

Ducking into the car, the door closed behind her, and she sipped the coffee. Nothing was as she expected. No sex but protection, a driver, and the perfect coffee. What game was McDade playing?

***

WORK HAD A WAY of focusing her. After too many hours in The Chronicler basement archives, she needed to get out of the building. If she didn't breathe fresh air at regular intervals, she got pretty myopic.

Outside, the Bentley was waiting. Just… waiting. Daly got out as she approached.

"I don't need the car. I'm going to a deli down the block," she said, looking up and down the street.

"Are you allowed to park there all day?"

"Think some beat cop's gonna challenge us?" Maybe. Maybe not. "Need me to come with you?"

"No," she said, smiling as she retreated. "You want anything?"

He shook his head, so she turned to lose herself in the bustle of people. They didn't matter. She was too in her own head. Facts and possibilities whizzed around in her mind.

McDade and Manzani. Maybe it wasn't wise to squeeze herself in between two families like theirs.

Her boss, Steeple, wanted her to build on the exposé piece she'd written about the Manzani family. Then her friend and source, Strat, tantalized her with a decades old McDade mystery. As an investigative reporter, she couldn't ignore the intrigue.

A McDade was missing. A McDade woman… and they were rare.

Connel's cousin. Did he know her? Remember her? She'd been gone a long time. Maybe they'd never met. Maybe she was long dead. And that was the mystery. What happened to Dorsey McDade?

In the deli, she ordered and sat at a table, all the while texting. Her brother. Strat. Steeple.

"Which one is it?"

The male voice drew her attention up, but the speaker was already sinking into the perpendicular chair.

"Evander," she said, every muscle tensing.

Evander "Vex" Manzani. Her not-so-secret admirer. Son of Don Silvio Manzani who ran most any part of the city Ire didn't.

"You get my flowers?" he asked, sliding a hand over hers. "You and your games, baby."

Why was he smiling?

Shit, that never led to anything good. "I'm not playing games." She withdrew from his touch. "How many times do I have to say it, Evander?"

"I love this play," he said, picking up her hand. "Shit, you love stirring it up. Staying all night at McDade's club…? Fuck, I thought you'd lost your mind, screwing that bastard. I'd fight that war for my princess, but talk about going nuclear."

"I'm not your princess," she said, dragging her hand from his again. "We've talked about this. This is not a game."

"That Irish scum…" he said like she hadn't spoken at all. "It's gotta be one of his guys… You want me to take them out one by one 'til I hit the one you fucked last night? I'll spill their blood for you. I'll play this out, right to the end."

His palm skimmed her arm; disgust prickled beneath it.

"Evander," she said, pacing a slow breath. "I don't want any blood spilled. What I was doing last night is none of your business. Are your people still following me?"

There was no other way he could know she'd spent the night at Stag.

"They expected you to come out. Every night you do… until last night. That fuck McDade is beneath you, beneath us, but his people… why the fuck…? Why degrade yourself? Is it blackmail? Have they got something on you? Why fuck with his guys?"

"I'm not. I wouldn't."

"McDade left with a blonde and a redhead after two," he said. Lucky women. "He know you were in his place fucking his guys?"

Keeping her face still, an odd curl of jealousy grew barbs in her belly. "Stop this. It isn't healthy for either of us."

"It's our curse," he said, his hand reaching the side of her neck. "Wanting each other."

"You can't keep doing this," she said. "Showing up like this. Someone will get hurt." Thank God Daly hadn't joined her or there would've been carnage. The deli people didn't deserve that. No one did. "Did you come in the front?"

If Daly saw…

"I know what you want," he said, dragging his chair closer, prompting her to look away. Why did he have to get so close? Sickness churned in her gut. When his lips touched her shoulder, she recoiled and whipped around, ready to lash out. But she couldn't. With a guy like Evander, there was a careful line to tread. "You want to keep it secret? Fuck with him behind his back?"

No, she really didn't, but this guy never heard her. "Evander—"

"This weekend, it's time to do this," he said. "Tomorrow night, Platinum Suite."

"What?"

He stood and bent over to kiss her hair. "Midnight."

Fading toward the back of the deli, he disappeared through an employee door.

Midnight. Friday. He wasn't suggesting… Except there, on the table by her coffee, was a key card bearing the Grand Hotel's logo.

Shit.

TWO

BACK IN THE archives that afternoon, putting together the McDade family tree complicated her attempts to rid Ire from her mind. Tough not to think about the guy when reading his name every twenty seconds.

Should she tell him about her conversation with Evander in the deli? Should she not? Ire assumed she'd chosen Stag for protection. Yes, fine, true. That didn't mean she'd ever intended for their paths to cross. Yet, somehow, not only had she got the McDades involved in her mess, but she'd ended up holding the detonator between the two factions.

Okay, so the families wouldn't be breaking bread anytime soon; that wasn't on her. But there was a tentative peace between the McDades and the Manzanis. Each had their own territories, their own strengths. They stayed away from each other's business as much as possible. By all outward appearances anyway.

How many news reports had she read that day? Hundreds? Thousands? However many it was, by the time she left The Chronicler building, it was dark out, and she didn't feel any wiser.

"Thought you'd ditched us again," Daly said, opening her car door. "Stag?"

"Home."

Before she could get in, he pushed the door to block her way. "Boss is expecting you."

And that was part of the deal.

"I'm hungry," she said. "And I'd bet he doesn't want me showing up without taking a shower and changing my clothes."

"An hour, max.," he said, determined, widening the ingress again.

"Did he say something?" she asked. "If he's giving you shit, just tell him the truth. I'm working. I have to do my job."

"This started as watching Manzani's mark."

One related to the other, how? "I don't—"

"Watching the boss's woman is a different gig. A whole different ballgame."

She smiled, ready to dismiss his concern. "Yeah, but it's not—"

Wait. Did Daly know about the deal? He had to know the relationship wasn't real. Didn't he? Hmm, best ask Connel and get some clarity on who knew what.

Daly stayed serious. "I have a job to do too."

Even if Daly was aware the relationship was a sham, others weren't. Did being Ire McDade's woman put her in a different kind of jeopardy? Avoiding Evander was one thing. Being queen in the hornet's nest was a new angle that could lead to worse trouble.

No one else should take heat for her choices. "I'll talk to him."

"You don't want to do that," he said.

"I don't?"

He shook his head and gestured inside. "Fifty-nine minutes."

Okay, right, he wanted to get moving. Now she did too. She and Ire needed to have a conversation.

***

THE EMBROIDERED NARROW straps of her red dress descended into a plunge that revealed her cleavage. It was just lucky she had a thing for buying dresses. Both her work and family lives required her to attend a bunch of functions, giving her plenty of excuses to splurge.

Haste. Yes, Daly wanted her to be quick. Still, things took as long as they took. More than an hour passed while she cooked, showered, and prettied herself for Stag. Her routine was the same as always… wasn't it? Okay, so she lingered over hair and makeup, and even did her nails. Either she cared about impressing Ire or was delaying the inevitable.

Both were probably true.

By the time the car pulled up to Stag, necessity drove her on. She got out with purpose in her step. How often was that purpose played through to the end? Never. Each time, Ire pulled the rug out from under her, and she ended up flat on her back. Literally. Being around him got her dizzy. Getting close… too close…

It wouldn't happen again. She'd have a drink, screw her head on straight, and complete her objective.

Guards at the foot of the stairs to the office moved aside, but her trajectory remained the same. Going straight past them, she strode on into the club. Something about the music grounded her. As always, the club delivered. Oblivion. Anonymity. Safe harbor.

Everyone needed to forget their lives sometimes. Forget who they were and everything going on around them. How could her life have become such a hot mess?

She ordered a drink and sat at the bar, pretending

nothing was different. Like she could just sit there, protected by the surrounding shell, the illusion of safety.

"Let me get that for you."

Fuck. A guy. A random guy. It never failed.

Her shoulders dropped as she exhaled. "No, thank you."

The guy, whoever he was, it didn't matter, sidled up close. Too close for a woman who wanted to be alone.

"Back up there, buddy."

Daly. He must've followed her because there he was, right behind her.

"Just talking to the lady."

"Yeah, you don't want to do that." Daly's arm came down on the bar between her and the guy she hadn't even looked at. "Back up."

"Who are you?" the guy asked. "She your girlfriend?"

Daly's head turned her way to murmur. "You don't want to do this, Sersha." The warning came in his words and his serious gaze. "They call him Ire for a reason."

"Hey, dude…" the guy said.

The bartender came over with her drink. "Daly, there a problem?"

Daly's eyes stayed on hers. "No problem, Biggs. Right, Sersha? Tell Biggs there's no problem."

Drawing in a breath, she picked up her drink. "No. No problem."

Her leash was short.

As she slipped off the stool, Daly's protective arm closed around her waist, guiding her through the tables, toward the exit again. But there was no reprieve. The security guys stepped out of the way to let them ascend the stairs toward the office.

"Playing with him isn't like playing with other guys," Daly hissed.

"I wasn't playing with anyone," she said. "Can't a girl just want a drink?"

"There's a fully stocked bar upstairs," he said, stopping at the top, holding the door handle. "You want a bartender up there? Just say the word." Their eyes met again. "But you cannot be around other guys like that. Women don't leave McDades. And you sure don't screw around on Ire McDade."

"Because Ire has a rep to protect?"

"Not for his sake."

"Mine?"

"Theirs," he said and edged in closer. "Shit, Sersha, you understand what he's capable of, right? He shot Dingo for walking in on you two together. What do you think a guy they call 'Ire' will do to any man who touches you? Who flirts with you? Who buys you a drink?"

Concern brought her brows closer. "Are you telling me to be afraid of him?"

"I'm telling you to be afraid *for* them. You want to fuck around with other guys? Their injuries, their deaths, will be on you."

She blinked in surprise. "Their deaths? You're exaggerating... aren't you?"

He snickered in contradiction. Someone pulled the door from his hand, opening it from the other side.

Niall stood there before them. "Just her. We're going out," he said to Daly, who turned to descend again. "Miss McLeod."

The acknowledgement came with Niall putting a hand on her lower back to push her inside. He closed the door behind her.

Ire was at the desk, on the phone, fixated on something in the corner. As she went a few steps, the long nook opposite his position opened up. The two blondes were on the chesterfield again. Sans clothes.

"Bring her…" Ire said into the phone, beckoning her with two straight fingers and pointing at the chair at the end of his desk. He smiled as his attention drifted, but it wasn't for her. "Make you no promises… I've heard…" She went to sit, putting the glass and her purse on the desk. "Not sure I do. Your Doherty puts on a show…" His light tone wasn't typical. Was it the blondes? Them enjoying each other seemed to be his focus. "I was there that night… Think every guy did…"

The blondes were beautiful, no denying it. Long silky hair. Perfect skin. What was it men enjoyed about women enjoying each other? Not that she judged them. Having never been with a woman, she couldn't say whether it would be satisfying to touch one like the pair on the couch touched each other.

Over the years, more than a dozen men had groped her. They'd used their hands and fingers to please her. She was used to men's bodies. The hard angles. The ridge of their arousal. How it felt to be filled by them.

The touch of his lips on her shoulder startled her. Was he finished on the phone? She tried to turn on a smile. With the women present, they couldn't talk about their situation, their deal, or about Evander.

Ire's narrow eyes stayed close, his lips a breath from her shoulder. What was it with men kissing her there?

Looking into him, a weight of need settled over her. Tired suddenly, but not in need of sleep, she licked her lips, aching to feel his against her again.

"Did I interrupt?" she asked, reaching for some semblance of sanity.

"My cousin."

That was a shock. The blondes, over there…

"They're your cousins?"

"On the phone," he said, sweeping her hair from her shoulder as he stood up.

Good, because that would be weird. Creepy… Perverted. They didn't look Irish either. Scandinavian? Russian? What did she know? Ire's father had dark hair. He looked just like him; she'd been looking at pictures of McDades all day. The women over there, kissing, touching, they didn't have the family's authority. Even in 2D, the McDades presented formidable figures.

Yet, something about the women entranced her. She couldn't tear her eyes away. Did they enjoy being on show? A hand on a breast slid lower. Sensing it, the second woman parted her thighs, moving into the caress.

"Want to join them?"

She jumped. How could she be unaware of him when he was her reason for being there?

His question filtered in and she breathed out an awkward laugh. "No. God, no."

"You're used to living with rules," he said, rounding the desk, whiskey in hand, to prop himself on the corner, observing the women too. "Those rules don't exist here, Sersha. Learn to be a bad girl. Satisfy your curiosity."

That lilt, the way he said her name, even that didn't quite land right. Mesmerized by the delicate fingers sliding through soft hair, the allure tempted her.

"I wouldn't—I mean I've never…" Her mouth dried. His glass landed on the desk, then his open hand was in front of her. "What?"

She slipped her hand into his and with one tug, he pulled her to her feet. His other hand drifted up her arm, along her clavicle to her throat.

"We don't need a reason to do something in this house," he said. The back of his finger ascended the front of her neck to ease her chin higher. He ducked to kiss her slow. No tongue, just a long, gentle press of his lips to hers. Her eyes stayed closed when his mouth ebbed. "We need a reason not to do it… No one expects you to be a good girl here. You don't need to behave. What reason is there to resist what feels good?"

THREE

HIS MOUTH GRAZED HERS. One kiss. And another. Taking more each time, he tempted her lips to part, sharing his breath as their tongues met.

The grate of her zipper descending razed the air.

She pulled away. "I can't," she whispered, grabbing for the edges of her dress beneath her arm.

"Because?"

"The first time… I trusted this because it felt so good."

"No cameras," he said, his hands curling around her waist, squeezing her so tight she had to straighten her posture to draw in more air. "No recordings. No audio. No video. Just us this time."

"Conn—"

"That's it," he murmured, crouching to kiss her again. "The way you say my name when you're turned on…" His palms descended as his fingers curled to gather her dress into his fists. "Fuck, baby, that's pleasure right there."

Really? "I trusted you before."

"You can trust me," he said. "Can I trust you?"

What did that mean? Trust her? She was… He stood on the opposite side of the tracks, wielding power over her and her family. But didn't she hold that same power? Damn, she hadn't even thought about it. Being so close to him, to his inner workings… He'd conducted business around her. She could've gone to her father about Babcock. Her brother. Connel wasn't the only one with leverage.

She could bring the McDade house tumbling down.

"The door's unlocked," she said, touching his face. "Being caught with you is one thing—"

"Lock it," he said. He'd let her do that? Lock his guards, his trusted advisors, out of the room? "Pleasure's the only rule, Ser."

So many pleasures. So many things she'd imagined doing with him. It was liberating. So freeing that it was almost funny. Usually people didn't take chains from her, they put them on. Would any of her exes have suggested anything even close to…?

"I'll embarrass myself."

"Not in my house," he said with a single head shake, resting his hands on her shoulders to push the straps down. "Dasha."

The command brought one blonde immediately to her feet. Wearing nothing but a smile, she came trotting over.

"Connel," she said, but he was already going to the door.

The snick of the key was unexpected. When he turned, their eyes met. Locking them in was a sign of reassurance and respect, which was… odd.

The blonde's hair tickled her arm before the heat of her soft lips touched the corner of her mouth. Connel was right there. Watching… Even on his approach, she was his focus.

Fingers linked between hers to guide her. Taking one step and another. Connel crossed behind them, heading for the desk.

The blonde, Dasha, guided her to the center of the rug as the second woman came to join them.

"I'm Darla," the second said, caressing her arm.

Dasha was forward about taking her arms from the dress, pushing it from her hips with her panties to expose her body. Darla directed her head around to steal her mouth. The kiss was different. Not bad different, just… less forceful, more playful. There was little authority in the way Darla kissed, though nothing tentative about it. Her tongue was faster, yet less intrusive. Smaller, maybe that was—

The warmth of hands on her breasts forced her away from the kiss. Dasha tossed her hair and bent to tickle her nipple with the tip of her tongue. Darla's mouth touched hers again.

Sensory overload stalled her processing. Darla was kissing her. Dasha's mouth was on her breasts, hands guided her hips, then she was down, sitting on cool leather with fingers in her hair, a tongue in her mouth. Another hand on her cheek pulled her head around. Someone's fingers slid up her thigh, but she clamped them together.

"Slow it down, ladies." Connel… somewhere in the room. "You've gotta learn to share."

Freed from the kiss, she swallowed hard, fighting to keep up with the panting of her breathing.

The hand escaped her thighs to tangle its fingers between hers.

"Can we go upstairs?" one woman asked.

"When she's ready," Connel said.

Between the women flanking her, caressing her body, she sought him. Perched against the front of the desk, whiskey in hand, there was something arousing about just having his eyes on hers.

Did she say his name differently when turned on? "Conn," she breathed, testing its depth on her tongue.

"While you're mine, this is your kingdom, baby." And maybe that was it, what he was showing her, that she could be free. Dasha and Darla might be intimate with each other, with him, but she hadn't seen any suggestion of a committed relationship. Did they know her association with Connel wasn't real? "Act like it."

Act like it… If she was his woman… If this was her safe place… A place she could do and say and be anything she wanted.

Tearing her eyes from him, she looked from one blonde to the other. They really were beautiful and must know what Connel liked. Maybe it wasn't about just pleasing him. There was power in it. A power that quaked inside her when she kissed Dasha.

It was real. That moment. It didn't mean anything, no more than the sweet need to experience something new. No one judged her. She was only doing what they'd done probably a hundred times before.

She could let them lead, be a passive player, or she could seize the moment.

Hadn't she come into Stag wishing for oblivion? Maybe that's exactly what the opportunity afforded her.

One arm wound around Darla. She stroked her back, felt the warmth of her hair in her fingers as her hand went higher. Switching her kiss to Darla, she pulled herself closer while caressing Dasha, squeezing her breast, enjoying the firm, soft flesh yielding to her grasp.

Dasha kissed her neck, the wet delight tingled on the surface of her sensitive skin. As her mouth got closer, Darla turned her head, kissing Dasha then her. In that moment, between them, the heat of excitement burned bright. The texture of their breasts on hers, their hair stimulating every part it touched. She'd never known hair was so arousing.

When she saw him again, her chest moving deep and slow, she could only think him being closer would enhance so much about the moment.

"Upstairs."

That bassy command ignited a surge of energy. Dasha and Darla leaped up, their hands linked in hers to guide her across the room fast. Trusting them to keep her going the right way, she twisted to look back for Connel.

He tossed the whiskey back in his throat and stalked after them. They weren't going up there alone. Maybe she'd get her wish.

Except as they ascended the stairs and flipped around to scurry toward the bedroom, trepidation cooled some of her need. She'd trusted him in that room before and it had come back to bite her.

Dasha and Darla were laughing as they climbed onto the bed, kissing before they'd even got as far as the pillows. Wrapped in each other, the women looked different in the dim light. Spread out there, on the black sheets, their delicate skin almost glowed.

His rough fingers skimmed onto her waist as he closed in behind her. Holding her in a half embrace, his caress continued to her breast.

"Trust me," he murmured above her ear.

Which was probably exactly what someone she shouldn't trust would say. "Will you join us?" she asked, her eyes closing as his touch got more demanding.

"I'll do what feels good," he said, still fondling her breast when he grabbed her hips to yank them back against his solid arousal. "Just like you."

"Come play," Dasha said, crawling away from Darla to snatch her hand and pull her down onto the bed.

What was she doing? Kissing one woman, the

other, pushing the first down to test more with her mouth. The smoothness of her jaw under her lips tempted her mouth lower. She kissed the swell of Dasha's breast and her nipple, enjoying how it reacted to the swirl of her tongue. Then she was on her back, Darla's body on top of hers, their breasts together, legs intermingled.

Kissing there, on her back in the bed, was easier than downstairs. Relaxing, hands could move, legs could open. This time when a feminine hand trailed across her hip, she pushed up into it. Fingernails grazed the seam of her leg. Not too long, but a new sensation. The push on her clit made her gasp; the circular stimulation sped and slowed. She hadn't even opened her eyes when the slick slide of a tongue on her pussy startled her.

Her eyes opened. Connel stood at the end of the bed. Naked. Cock in hand. Fuck. While her pussy was being spoiled by two women, he was enjoying the view in the most intimate, exposing way.

"Connel..." she breathed, undulating against the pleasure being gifted to her.

His gaze locked on hers and he shook his head. It wasn't enough. Petulant in her annoyance, she wanted to toss aside the women and beg him to fill her up. She needed it. More than them, she needed him.

It was selfish. She was being selfish. Everyone was in the moment, enjoying what felt good, and her focus was on what she was being denied.

Determined not to ruin what everyone else reveled in, she sat up. Pushing the women from their feast, she gripped Dasha's hair, pulling her mouth up to share the taste the blonde had been enjoying. Her. That sweet nectar belonged to her, and Darla wanted in on the action, taking one kiss and another.

Easing Dasha onto her back, she took the kiss and guided the two women's mouths together as she took advantage of the chance to know the taste of another woman. Kissing Dasha's body as her own had been kissed, she rubbed her cheek against the woman's breast and kept going south, trailing a hand down Darla's body as Dasha's legs parted.

The open invitation lured her curious mouth. She kissed, licked, rolled her tongue around Dasha's clit and the beauty's moan encouraged her. It was power. Going down on a guy was empowering too, but there was something so much more vulnerable about a woman in the throes of passion. Something much more giving too. With guys she was giving, and they were all about the taking, which was fine. That's how she thought it went. But Dasha was giving even in the way she moved her hips, in the whispers of gratitude that escaped her lips.

Darla joined her, kissing the center of their third, touching their tongues even as she teased Dasha's opening. Her curiosity was alive, captivated, lost in the moment of exploration. It was only the certainty of that hand on her hip that reminded her of the pleasure she craved.

When his blunt head probed her folds, her head rose just a fraction. It was impossible not to push back into that offering. She wanted it. More than her other lovers, more than her intrigue. He kept hold of her hip in one hand, his cock just there, resting against its goal. He couldn't be so cruel, could he? Couldn't tease her with proximity and withhold the drug she needed?

Dasha's pants and squeals grew louder, but her own head just rested there on the woman's thigh as Darla did the real work.

Grabbing her other hip, he surged forward. A spear of climax and agony shot through her.

She rose onto her knees, grasping for his hand on her hip.

"Conn," she gasped, pleading with him as her

back hit his body.

She tried to twist, to seek his mouth, but it was Dasha's that found hers. The women kissed her, each other, but it was the man driving in and out of her that got her body glowing, her heart racing.

It was his hands she wanted on her breasts, not Darla's mouth. Dasha was going lower, her tongue slid against her clit. But it didn't last. Connel propelled into her, using the strength in his grip to move her hips fast. His other arm came around her, pulling her back to him, pushing Dasha's head away from her body.

She couldn't even think as she dropped to catch her weight on her straight arms. Dasha and Darla were down there, sort of beneath her, entertaining each other as the mass of orgasm built, stealing her breath, her sense, her wits. All she wanted was that. Him inside her, hammering hard, racing toward his own end.

"Connel!" she screamed when climax hit hard.

She sucked in a breath and braced; still static, immobile as the world kept spinning. He slid out of her, and she dropped onto the bed, slowing her breathing. In the middle of the bed, the blondes remained wrapped in each other. Neither noticed Connel enter the bathroom. She did.

Was he finished or was a blonde next? She didn't want to watch that. Stupid as that was. He'd just watched the three women together and encouraged her to be free. Still, how would she feel witnessing him pleasuring another woman?

FOUR

HER BODY MOVED as she opened her eyes and there were his, just a few inches away.

"Connel," she said, her voice hoarse. What a night… What did she remember? Oh, it took effort to rouse herself to check the bed. "Just us?"

"Extras don't stay the night," he said.

The sheet was over her breasts, but his torso was bare. Shit. Ripped wasn't a strong enough word. Every ridge and groove threatened to torment her tastebuds.

"I'm not an extra?"

"Not as far as the world's concerned."

The world? Shit. Light shone from the living room into the doorless room.

She sat up, holding the sheet to her chest. "The world," she gasped the words. "Oh my fucking God, the world."

Forgetting modesty, she scrambled for the end of the bed.

"I can get 'em back with a call, baby," he said. "Relax."

She looked left to right, searching the floor and coming up short. Her clothes… damnit, they'd be downstairs.

Suddenly, he grabbed her wrist to yank her down to the bed, on her back, him on her.

"Conn—"

He kissed her. Not gentle or slow, he was already massaging her breast, opening her legs with his.

She pushed at him. "Don't," she said, but he kissed her chin, her throat, that sensitive spot just above her collarbone. "I have to get out of here."

"Fuck your boss," he said, stroking his lips left to right on her breast. "My guys will go over there. Talk to him."

"Steeple doesn't care," she said, trying to ignore the coil of enticement his mouth left in its wake. "Your guys are still here, right? Some of them must stay somewhere on the premises. The whole basement thing…" Thank God he was busy with her navel. "Which one of them could be fucking me?"

That didn't come out right, not that she realized until his dark eyes appeared above hers.

"I'll tolerate other women on my terms," he said, glaring. "Any guy touches you, I'll gut him myself…" The depth of his certainty clung to her, but damn if her hips didn't tilt to push her pussy against him. His brow twitched. "You bloodthirsty, baby? Fuck, you're with the right guy."

No, but it gave her an answer about that night. Her heart sped up, thumping hard between them. She had to close her eyes, to stop looking into his, to break the connection.

Fighting was useless.

His lips touched hers again, stealing more of her sense. How could she resist?

Digging her nails into his shoulders, she

desperately wanted to pull him closer, to wrap her arms around him in the same way her legs coiled around his hips.

Her lips parted, freeing a moan. The damage had been done. Maybe if they were quick—

"Boss!"

He punched the bed by her head, thrusting himself up. "Fuck off!"

"Shh," she murmured, cupping his jaw, guiding his mouth back to hers. His cock was full, imprinting itself on her, though not in the right place. She'd never hated being shorter than a partner more. Running her fingers into his hair, she rolled her mouth from his. "Protection?"

"I got it," he said, his hand shifting on the bed.

"Boss?"

Another holler, definitely wary.

He tore his kiss away. "I'll rip his fucking throat out," he hissed through gritted teeth.

"It's okay," she whispered, stroking his face, pained by the fury in him. "Baby…"

His anger ebbed when their eyes met. She hadn't called him that before… had she?

"Boss?"

Less of a shout, the voice was closer.

Connel turned his head in that direction. "You trying to lay eyes on my lady?"

"No! No, boss…"

"Conn," she said, though wasn't sure if she was teasing or scolding.

"Niall and Daly got hit," the guy from beyond said.

Snap, the mood changed.

Connel pounced to an elbow to check behind them, then was on his feet. "When?" he called, striding into the closet. "Stay out of the fucking bedroom."

Why? Because she was lying naked in his bed? Hadn't her plan been to leave?

"Less than an hour ago," the guy called.

Connel came out clothed only to disappear into the living room. "In daylight?"

The men's voices faded as their footsteps disappeared down the stairs.

Fixating on the ceiling, she considered going after him to share Evander's warning. But she just lay there. Someone fucked up… and, chances were, it was her.

FIVE

"I SCREWED UP last night," she said, striding past Strat to go into his apartment before he had time to register who'd knocked.

In the living room, she tossed her purse at her usual chair, but didn't sit. Too much frantic energy buzzed inside her, so she paced instead.

"What'd you do, Scamp?" Strat asked, yawning as he approached.

She stopped. "I had sex with Connel McDade." Shock flattened his affect. For about ten seconds, he said nothing. The silence was too excruciating to tolerate. "Actually, I had sex with two random women and Connel McDade."

He backed up into the kitchen to put coffee and water in the machine before turning and laying his hands on the breakfast bar.

"Four of you? He was the only dude?" She shrugged. "Damn, why'd I get out of the game? He hiring?"

"Strat…" she said and went over to lean on the

counter opposite him. "Evander approached me yesterday. At lunch. He knew I spent Wednesday night over there."

He frowned. "Over where?"

"Stag."

"Shit," he said. "You're seeing Ire McDade? How long?"

It was on the tip of her tongue to tell him the truth. But it was against the rules… Connel's rules.

"Just this week," she said, because it was true. "We met at Stag."

Also true.

"What were you doing at Stag?" he said. "Hiding from Manzani? Shit, Scamp. Avoiding one asshole, you get yourself mixed up with another?"

"This isn't about that," she said, going around the counter into the tiny kitchen with him. "Evander's people have to still be watching because he knew I stayed over… he thought I was screwing one of Connel's guys."

"You weren't. You were screwing him."

Not that night, but that was irrelevant. "Evander thinks it's a game. That I'm teasing him or something."

"Vex Manzani thinks everything you do is to tease him."

"Right, except Evander's made a reservation… at a hotel. He wants me to meet him there tonight."

"Scamp—"

"I know," she said, hearing his warning tone. "I can't. I mean, I wouldn't."

"They'll kill each other. Don't put two guys like them up against each other."

"I didn't mean to do that. It wasn't my intention. I told Conn I didn't need protection from Evander, but it snowballed and now…" Her hand rose to her throat. "Something happened this morning. Someone hit Connel's guys… I didn't get specifics, but—"

"You think it was Vex? That this is because of you?"

"Maybe."

He took cups from a cabinet and filled them with coffee. "What did McDade say when you told him?" Sucking her lower lip into her mouth, she salved it with her tongue. When there was no reply, he looked back at her. "You told him… You did tell him?"

Exasperated frustration burst out of her. "How can I do that?" she asked. "Maybe I'm wrong."

"Maybe you're right. Vex could pick McDade's guys off one by one. When do you say stop? And what do you plan to do tonight? Go to the hotel with Vex?"

"No!"

"Stag with Ire? What happens when Vex finds out you're not coming? Is he going to show up at the club?"

That would be horrific. People would get hurt.

"If I tell Conn, it'll start a war."

On an exhale, he put his cup down. "You want to cut them both out? I don't know who could protect you against two guys like them, with their resources, their armies. Your brother would try—"

"I don't want my family involved." Hence how she got into the mess in the first place. "What do I do?"

"You're not going to like it," he said, resting a shoulder on the fridge.

"What? Help me out, Strat."

"Loyalty's the only weapon. You've gotta pick a guy and go all in."

"I can't do that." Because one relationship wasn't real and the other repulsed her. "I can't."

"Alternative is walking away from both. You pulled the pin. What you meant to happen doesn't matter. No one gives a shit about intentions. You're in it. Abandoning them both is risky. You could end up the focus of their anger. Embarrassing and disrespecting both of them would be crazy. Hell, that might unite them against you. Trust one of them, take the risk on one of them. It's the only way out."

"And if Conn blames me?" She worried about the injured men. Daly had been good to her. She didn't want him hurt. "Then what?"

"If he's going to blame you, he'll blame you now or later. The truth will get out eventually; it always does." Man, she hoped not. There were too many truths she wanted to keep secret. "If he finds out you were lying to him the whole time…"

"Okay," she said, balling her determined fists at her sides. "So we have another problem."

"What?"

She winced. "I don't know where to find him at this time of day."

He almost rolled his eyes. "I'll make some calls," he said, picking up one coffee to hand it over as he disappeared into his bedroom.

She should've told Connel that morning. Should've found out the condition of his people. Except by the time she tiptoed down to his office, it was empty. She hadn't seen anyone and had left without security opening the door or a car waiting at the curb.

Strat was right. Coming to him, sounding off was a good plan. Now she just needed to figure out what to tell Connel… If he was in the mood to hear her.

SIX

"YOU KNOW THIS outs us," she said to Strat in the driving seat.

"Can't let you walk in there alone, Scamp," he said. "Think I want to read your obit tomorrow?"

"He's not going to hurt me."

"I set up the meet," he said. "They know this is coming from me." Did they know she was with him? "I told you I can go in there alone."

"And how would you possibly know Evander came to me?"

"Like you said, he and Ford used to run in the same circles."

"No," she said, shaking her head. "I don't want your family involved." If she didn't want hers at risk, why should she risk Strat's? "He might get mad. I know he has a short fuse."

Strat glanced at her. "And you want to walk in there alone?"

"I'm more worried about you. I don't want you to get hurt."

"I've been dealing with guys like McDade my whole life. I might be old enough to be your dad, but I ain't passed it yet."

"Guess I can always tell him you're senile or something."

"Ha ha," he drawled at her smile. "You kids think you invented this shit."

She could joke about Strat's age, but he was sharper than most young guys and still took care of himself. He'd been in his mid-teens when Ford, his eldest kid, was born, still just a kid himself. She wouldn't count Strat out of any situation. If nothing else, his experience was useful.

They stopped outside Stag. She'd woken up there that morning. Been in and out more times than she'd counted. Until that moment, she'd never been nervous.

"Wait there," Strat said and got out to come around and open her door.

It wasn't a limo, so unfortunately, it didn't come with liquor. She could use a little liquid courage.

On the sidewalk, Strat surprised her by taking her hand. Physical contact wasn't typically their gig. Maybe it was weird because her own father would never do something so reassuring.

The door opened as they approached and Strat took her inside, tucking her behind him as they passed the stairs she expected them to ascend. But they didn't. They went down the corridor and into the main club.

Five guys stood dotted around the room. That she could see anyway. Strat stopped just a foot inside, blocking most of her view.

"Always did have more balls than brains, Strat." A voice she recognized, but not Connel's. Niall's. At least that was confirmation he had his life. "Thought you were out of the game. You're the last person we expected to call."

"Yeah," Strat said. "Came here for Ire."

"You get me. Talk."

He tugged her hand, pulling her out from behind him. "Who does she get?"

Niall was on a stool at the bar until he saw her.

Sliding off the seat, he widened his stance. "Shit, Strat, you're suicidal."

"Just wanna talk."

"You hit our guys, then kidnap the boss's girl? What the fuck is wrong with you?"

"He didn't kidnap me," she said, and tried to walk, but Strat held her back. "It's okay."

"He's not even here," Strat said to her. "You talk to Ire, Scamp. Only Ire."

Because how could she trust his people? She didn't know Niall at all. She knew Daly better. Which reminded her.

"How's Daly?" she asked Niall. "Is he okay?"

"In a bad way," Niall said. "That what you wanted?"

"This wasn't me," she said, turning her desperation on Strat because maybe it was her. "Maybe I should leave the country."

"And go which way?" he asked, a semi-smile tilting his lips. "They have people everywhere."

True, and that left her with… what? She couldn't tell Lachlan. Wouldn't be able to face his disappointment. Somehow that stung more than her father or grandfather's.

A voice uttering foreign words rose behind the wall at the back of the bar. What was back there? A man. Although she didn't understand the speech, she recognized the signature.

Connel.

He appeared around the far corner of the bar, approaching behind Niall with a couple more guys following. Niall responded in a similar tongue and retreated behind his boss.

"Talk," Connel said, his gaze flicking from her to Strat and back. "You're out of your depth, old timer."

"Old fucking…" Strat grumbled. "I was hustling this city while you were spunk in your daddy's balls, boy. And your old man? He was a fucking asshole." Laying a hand on his arm, she didn't want Strat to dig himself a pit. "But you know what would never happen in your daddy's day? Your father would never have his woman trapped, in fear for her life, while he sat with his thumb up his ass."

"Strat," she whispered, moving closer. Her friend didn't know the relationship wasn't real. That wasn't his fault, but challenging Connel wasn't smart regardless. "This is not on him."

"Anyone hurts her…" Connel said, "they have me to deal with."

"Right," Strat said, putting an arm around her. "Guess that's why she had to come to me. 'Cause a real man gets involved before their woman gets hurt." He pulled her against him, backing up a step. "Let's get out of here. I don't want you near either of them."

What could she do? How could she resist?

"Either?" Connel asked.

"You know why she came here in the first place," Strat said, pausing mid-turn. "Why she was in this club. You think that problem just evaporated?"

"She's protected."

When Strat laughed, she laid a hand on his chest and looked up, but his glare remained fixed on the other side of the room. On the man she'd woken up with.

"Yeah, that's why she's got an appointment in his bed tonight… guess at least it saves her from yours."

"Stop," she murmured, pushing on him, though his arm stayed around her. "Don't antagonize him. I don't want this. I never wanted this."

"She won't go near—"

"What choice does she have?"

"Stop!" she said, shoving Strat hard to free herself and put some space between them. "Both of you, this is ridiculous." She exhaled, composing herself before meeting Strat's eye. "We knew this was a risk. We took it. It didn't work out." She turned to Connel. "We're sorry we wasted your time." She could mention the tape, but that was the least of her worries when lives were at stake. "I'd appreciate it if you gave Daly my best." Returning to Strat, she took his hand again. "Let's go."

"Sersha." Maybe it was the authority in Connel's tone that did it. On instinct, she stopped. Was he going to threaten them? Suddenly, there were footsteps and a door closed. After a beat, he asked, "Can I trust you?" That was what he'd asked her last night. Was it a threat? Spinning around, she locked her gaze on him. "I haven't lied to you yet."

As he'd said the night they made their deal. Ask him a question…

They were alone. Her. Him. Strat and Niall. They were the only four present. Those eyes, their intensity, their promise…

"Evander came to me at lunch yesterday."

Though he tried to hide it, she saw anger flash behind his façade. "Where was Daly?" he asked, his lips barely moving.

"I was in the deli just down the block from work. I told Daly not to come. I didn't think that… Evander came in the back." At least he'd left that way, so she assumed he'd arrived that way too. "I don't know if it's… He knew I slept over here on Wednesday night… he assumed I was screwing one of your guys."

"Which one of them could be fucking me," he muttered her words from earlier.

"Right," she said.

"That was your panic this morning. You think his people are watching the club."

"They must be," she said. "I thought so long as he didn't know it was you, it would be okay. He seems to think that…"

"Gets him going when she plays with him," Strat said, laying a supportive hand on her shoulder. "He doesn't get she's not interested."

"In his head, it's not even a possibility someone wouldn't want him," she said, "that a woman wouldn't want him. He's used to getting whatever he wants."

"This has been going on since she was nineteen," Strat said. "He comes and goes any way he fucking pleases."

"That doesn't matter," she said, putting a hand over Strat's on her shoulder. "It wouldn't, but… It's different now."

"People are getting hurt," Strat said. "Your guys today."

"I don't know if it was anything to do with him."

"Convenient he threatens your guys and they get hit the next day."

"What was the threat?" Niall asked.

Connel absorbed everything. He wasn't speaking, didn't move, he just sat there saying nothing.

She breathed out. "He asked if I wanted him to take out your guys one by one until he hit the one I was screwing."

Niall barked, "And you didn't fucking tell—"

Connel raised a hand to silence his subordinate. "Did you tell him we're together?"

"No!" she said. "The last thing I want to be responsible for is a war between your families. The Irish and Italians aren't known for playing nice. Evander finds out… if he ever found out… He can't find out. Ever.

He's not stable. He's unhinged. He has no right, but he'll come for you. I can't stop him, and I can't be responsible for… This shouldn't even be on your radar."

It shouldn't be on anyone's radar. Who knew one conversation almost seven years ago would lead them all to this point?

A few seconds passed. Probably a few seconds. It felt like three hours. Scrutinizing him, she waited for a question, for an answer, for any acknowledgement or hint of what was in his head. Then it moved, just a fraction, and she slipped away from Strat to cross to the man who'd gestured for her.

SEVEN

"SER…" Strat warned from behind.

Focused, caught in the tractor beam stare of the man propping himself on a barstool, she couldn't resist. Yeah, he could hurt her, but she wasn't afraid.

When she reached him, Connel took her hips to guide her into the vee of his parted thighs. Rather than say a word, his lips came to hers. Closing her eyes, she relaxed against him, folding her arms between them, appreciating the shield of his body. His hands slid up her back to lose themselves in her hair, gripping it tighter as the need of his kiss grew.

As she was losing herself in him, he tore his mouth away. Was the kiss for the benefit of others? Sometimes it was easy to forget they weren't a real couple. Thinking that way could be dangerous, could get her hurt.

"You tell me everything," he murmured on her, tightening his fists in her hair. "And you don't leave my side from now on."

"We can't be together all the time," she said, her

heart still pumping. "My family can't—"

"Shit," he said, his head turning.

Disappointing him didn't feel good. It shouldn't matter, but it did. Throwing up obstacles between them annoyed her. His fists loosened in her hair, combing it out as his arms relaxed around her.

Resting her head against his, she angled to kiss his jaw. "I'm sorry."

He scooped her hair into one hand, using it to pull her head back. "You trust Strat?"

She blinked up at him. "I don't want him to get hurt."

"I don't want you to get hurt."

"Maybe this morning was nothing to do with yesterday," she said, slipping her hands under the collar of his shirt, seeking skin. "Maybe it's just a coincidence. You're in a dangerous line of work—"

"Payback for this morning comes after payback for yesterday," he said and frowned, saying something else in his mother tongue that she didn't understand. His expression darkened as his fingers found hers to guide them down inside his shirt. "You have a responsibility to the family."

His stag head tattoo was under her fingertips. Reading the ferocity of his glare was difficult. Did he mean it? Was he pissed he'd put his name near hers when the Manzanis were causing shit? She'd endangered his men. Whether or not Evander targeted them, the possibility existed. She should've warned him. Given him a chance to defend himself.

"Approaching your woman is a personal slight," Niall muttered. "You can't let the guys do it."

"No," she said, curling her fingers into a fist on her lover. "I don't want you going near him. If you hurt him, he'll hurt you back."

"Worried about him?"

"No," she said, unintimidated by his scorn, "but where does it end? You hit him, he hits you back. If you challenge him—"

"Enough," he said, threading their fingers together as he stood. "Strat, she doesn't leave your sight unless she's with me."

"Hey, I didn't—"

"You can't ask him to—"

"Put him on payroll," Connel said over his shoulder to Niall and started across the room, taking her with him.

"Connel," she said. "Conn…"

He didn't slow, just kept on going, across the width of the club to a spiral staircase almost beneath where the office would be. They went up onto a balcony she'd never noticed and through a door into… the apartment living room. How had she never registered the door there before? Because it was dark? Because she was always in a heady state of mind?

"Don't contradict me in front of anyone," he said, dropping her hand to turn to her. "Ever."

"No?" she asked, her hands rising to her hips. "Guess again! I will contradict you if you're talking crap. How can you even think about going near Evander Manzani? How can you ever—"

Grabbing her jaw, he slammed her against the wall. "You will not contradict me," he snarled.

Why wasn't she afraid? With Evander she feared for her virtue, hell, she feared for her life. But there, alone with this glaring man, the guy renowned for his temper, she wasn't scared.

"You'll get yourself killed," she said, locked in his hold. "What will happen to your precious family then?" Shoving away from her, he turned his back. "It doesn't even make sense. Why would you want to go after him? Risk a war between your families for the woman you're blackmailing into bed. Your ego is not that fragile. You shouldn't give a shit—"

"It's about pride," he said without turning. "One man takes another's woman—"

"That what it is? He touched your toy? Goddamnit, you—"

"He touched you?" he roared, spinning around to bear down on her. "Where?"

"It doesn't matter," she snapped back, but laid calming hands on his chest, switching to a soothing tone. "You have to control your anger."

He swiped her hands away. "Where?"

Screaming at each other wouldn't change what had been. Anything she said would likely only inflame tensions further.

With her hands flat on the wall at her sides, she rose on her tiptoes to brush her lips across his. Encouraged that he didn't run away, she did it again. This time when he grabbed her jaw, he squeezed it tight and forced it higher, opening her mouth to plunge his tongue against hers.

Wet heat pushed his kiss deeper. Frantic. Fast. Devouring. Suddenly starved, both were desperate in their need. The moment she touched his belt, his other arm scooped her up, holding him to her as they crossed the room.

Maybe they crossed the room. She didn't know anything but the consuming taste of the mouth fighting hers. It wasn't dominance. No, he had superiority in sex, and she gave it of her own freewill. Both wanted something, they needed what they could only get from the other.

They fell to the bed, their lips never parting. Not until his trekked down her throat.

"Conn…" she begged, raising her hips.

He ripped open her shirt and dropped to kiss her

stomach, running his hands up over her breasts. She loosened her skirt, kicking off her shoes, working to rid the fabric from her body. Desperation in their desire, like someone or something could steal them from each other any second, their urgency ratcheted up.

"Please…" she pleaded, pushing on his shoulders. His mouth kept on going until his tongue was on her clit. When his finger slipped into her, she yelped. "Oh, Conn…"

"You're wet," he panted, rising to kiss her again. "Hot for me, baby?"

He had no idea, not if he was wasting time with words. "You enjoy it," she whined, undulating against his probing digit. "Torturing me."

"You accused me of it the night we met," he said, running his tongue along her lower lip.

"Stop talking and fuck me, McDade!"

His lips curled as he reached between them to open his pants. She helped unbuckle his belt and wasn't even surprised when he tore open the rubber with his teeth. The guy must take protection literally everywhere.

Her belly clenched when he pushed into her. "Conn," she hissed, her head going all the way back as her body responded to his.

There was no easing in. He took her hard and fast, filling and depriving her in such swift strokes, she was still panting his name in grief as he returned to his place inside her. Sex wasn't supposed to feel like that, it wasn't supposed to feel like the answer to every question in the universe.

Fear? Worry? None of it meant anything. This was all there was.

As her eyes opened to his determination, her hand rose to his face. So much satisfaction came in pleasing the man, in giving herself to him with such open abandon, no barriers stood between them.

For the first time in her life, a brief flash of resentment toward their condom only enhanced her pleasure. That was how much she wanted to belong to him, how much she longed to be the only one beneath him, offering him shelter and acceptance.

"Macushla," he panted, his control ragged in the growl of his voice. "Ser…"

"I'm with you, baby," she gasped, grabbing for the back of his neck. "Shit, Conn! I'm—"

His long growl came with a thrust that hit her so deep, she felt it in every trembling nerve.

"Conn…" she sighed, her palm moving to his cheek.

"I need you to tell me…" he said, breathing hard. "You need to tell me the truth."

"I will," she said. "I know I should've said something this morning—"

"No," he said, taking her hand from his face as he dropped onto his back beside her. Flattening her palm on his chest, he rolled his head on the pillow to meet her eye. "How far did you go with him?"

Evander again already. Had he been on her lover's mind the whole time they were screwing?

"In the deli? He took my hand and—"

"Has he fucked you?"

"No," she said, propping herself on an elbow. "No! Conn, we've never even kissed. Not…" Swaying his way, she pressed her mouth to his. "It's so different…" Sliding her hand out from beneath his on his chest, she unbuttoned his shirt. "I was nineteen when we met. A bunch of us got fake IDs and ended up in one of the Manzani clubs. I can't even remember now if we knew that." She semi-shrugged, opening his shirt to stroke his torso. "I probably did. My dad was in the organized crime division for years… We were partying, thought we were all that and…"

"He hit on you?"

"Yeah," she said, watching her fingers caress his flesh. "He came over with so much swagger… He was a kid then too, I guess, twenty-something, mid-twenties. He was probably used to getting every girl he winked at. All the guys with him, they hooked up with my friends… I ended up calling Lach for a ride home. He'd always said I could call no matter what, and he said nothing in the car, but…"

Relaxing onto her back again, she covered her eyes. What was she doing? All he'd wanted to know was if she and Evander ever slept together. Of course he needed to know that if he was going to confront the guy.

"But what?" he asked, scooping her breast from her bra cup.

His mouth was around her nipple when her hand dropped from her face. "You don't care," she said, sitting up to take off her shirt and bra only to lie back down. "It doesn't matter. Point is, Evander didn't get lucky. He never got lucky with me. We've never made out. No first base, second base, nothing—"

"But what?" he asked, his eyes on hers though he massaged her breast. "McLeod said nothing, but…?"

"You don't have to confront Evander about the deli," she said. "Not on my behalf. I understand you want to protect your people, you should. I know you're responsible for them and I apologize they got caught up in this, that you got caught up in this. I told you I didn't need protection and I meant it."

"We're so far past that point," he said, sitting up. "You'll move in here—"

"I'm not moving in here," she said, sitting up as he rose from the bed to go into the closet. "I can't live here. How will that help? Do you have men who live here full time?"

"Stag is completely secure."

"That's not what I'm worried about," she said. "Unless you plan to set one of your guys up to take the heat, Evander will keep coming for your people."

For as long as she and Connel were involved anyway. As long as she kept visiting Stag and staying the night.

"It's Friday," he called out.

Scooching to the edge of the bed, she wrapped the sheet around her body. "Which means?"

"He'll be in Hustle all night."

"Hustle…" she murmured to herself, then shot to her feet to storm into the closet. "His sex club? You want me to go to his sex club?"

"You're not going anywhere," he said, typing on his phone. His shirt was gone, his pants still open. "Dasha will be here in twenty minutes. She's got a card; get whatever you need new. Manzani will be watching your place, avoid it. Avoid tipping our hand."

"I can't live under siege," she said, going closer. "And you can't shut me out. I caused this…" Right in front of him, she still didn't get his attention. "Can I see Daly? I need to apologize."

He looked at her. "He's at the doc's."

"A hospital?"

"With a guy on payroll."

And she could argue with him, but things worked differently in his world. She'd studied it, talked about it, read, learned, but this was her first time living it that deep.

"This'll never work," she said, laying a hand over the phone to stop it distracting him.

"It's under control."

"I can't live here, Connel. I have an apartment."

"I can't secure it like I can Stag. You have an army here."

"Is this your pride again? You just can't be

incapable, can you? My family won't understand. They'll ask questions. And my boss? What about my work? I'm in the middle of an investigation."

"Baby, don't worry about work," he said. "My guys will go over there—"

"To scare the shit out of my boss?" she asked and smiled. "Steeple is a good guy. He takes care of his people."

"Not that good. You're mixed up with me and Vex."

EIGHT

IF ONLY SHE could blame someone else for her predicament. Unfortunately, no one else was culpable, not even by association.

"Vex happened years before I started working for Steeple," she said. "And ending up here was my fault… I got tired of sitting in my apartment waiting for him to knock."

"Another reason you're living here."

"I have to be able to do my job. How would you feel if I got between you and your work?"

"That's what you're doing now," he said, backing up to go into the bathroom with her close behind.

He turned on the shower and shirked his pants to step under the spray. As the steam rose, obscuring her view, the idea of joining him appealed.

Until voices interrupted her fantasy. "Could be he killed her."

"Don't count her out. She's scrappy."

That second one was Strat.

Leaving Connel, she went into the living room as

Strat and Niall got to the top of the stairs.

"You reach an agreement?" Niall asked her.

Strat was checking out her apparel or lack of it. "Looks like she reached something else."

He hadn't missed her purse scaled across the floor either. Somehow that had become a victim of their passion and she couldn't even remember it leaving her hand.

"Better that than fighting," she said, tucking the sheet in over her breasts. "Either of you want a drink?"

"Making yourself at home, Scamp?"

"If Conn has his way, I'll never leave," she said, delighted to find a coffee machine and sink behind the bar.

"Where is he?"

"Shower," she said, switching on the machine.

"You've got to keep your head," Strat said, sitting on a stool at the other side of the bar. "Keep thinking straight."

"The truth is, it's out of my control," she said, figuring out the machine.

"Yeah, neither will take orders."

"That's her job."

Everyone turned to Connel's voice coming toward them from the bedroom. New pants, shirt, all put together, though his hair was damp. Mmm, damn, she should've joined him.

Her finger jumped to grind the beans, seeking purpose.

"Want to hit the club?" Niall asked Connel when the machine was done.

"Hustle will be stacked to the rafters tonight," Strat said. "If the McDades go in there for you, Scamp… You'll hit the headlines."

Continuing with the coffee, she retrieved a cup. "I don't want to hit headlines or anyone to hit anything.

Evander won't be at Hustle tonight."

"Not all night, sure," Strat said. "But he might go early. Hang out until—"

"You think he'll spend the evening having sex with other women before meeting me for sex?"

Hardly adoring. Insulting, actually, given he claimed to care about her.

Strat snickered. "Apparently, you don't mind sharing."

She couldn't even look at Connel or Niall.

"Thanks," she said. "Makes the night real special. After waiting years to be with me, he gifts me an STD on our first night together." She faked an insincere swoon. "How romantic."

When he laughed again, she joined in and poured the coffee.

"What is that?" Niall asked. "Your first night together?"

"His parting gift at lunch yesterday," Strat said. "He told her to meet him in a hotel tonight."

"Tonight?" Connel said. "The appointment's real?"

"It's no big deal," she said, taking the first espresso down the bar to put it in front of him. "I never intended to go."

"Naw," Niall said. "But means we know where he'll be…" His focus went to his boss. "Alone."

"He won't be alone," Strat said. "Vex doesn't go anywhere alone. Guy's shit scared of his own shadow. Growing up with brothers like his, don't think he ever threw a punch. Why'd you think my boy and his crew were always at his back? Not 'cause they loved him, 'cause he needed them. Security will be there."

"In the room?" she asked, shocked at the idea of performing with a live audience.

"Outside the room," Strat said and shrugged.

"Or inside, whatever you prefer, I guess. I'm sure McDade's got guys who'll watch if that's your—"

"Let's stop talking about this," she said, going back to the machine to repeat the process. "It's weirding me out. I get a physical reaction when I think about it."

"Think about what?" Strat asked. "Screwing?"

"Screwing Evander Manzani," she said. "I should get a medal. Seven years avoiding a guy's cock has got to be some kind of record."

"I'm amazed he's let you avoid it," Strat said. "I know some of the shit he's done to women who—"

She hit the button to grind the beans, cutting him off while showing him a broad smile. The prospect of force would terrify any woman. Sometimes that possibility kept her up nights. Any time there was a noise, or she spooked herself, Evander was her first thought. He could force himself into her apartment, into her bed, whenever he chose. There, but for the grace of God went she.

As soon as the machine stopped, Niall spoke, "Why didn't ya tell him to fuck hisself?"

"Because she likes her head on her neck," Strat said. "You should be impressed, not judgmental. Woman's kept herself alive and out of his bed. We guys came up with crews at our backs, we walked with armies. Scamp here's on her tod… as you would say."

"She's got daddy, granddaddy—"

"Please, you ever met either of them? Seen the way they talk to her?"

"Strat," she said, trying to soothe and prevent him from ramping up.

"No, if he's gonna blame you for Vex's shit, he should know what he's talking about. Her daddy and granddaddy disagree with how she lives her life and blame her for everything too. You'd get along swell."

When Strat rose, Niall did too. Shit, this couldn't

come to blows. Abandoning the coffee machine, how the hell would she stop—

"Hold," Connel said, cool and calm. Although it pained or pissed off the others, their shoulders did drop a little. He put an arm out to stop her passing him. "Niall, get Strat introduced to the guys on tonight. They need to know his position." Niall turned to glare at him. "Or we take this to the basement, but you know how that ends."

"Fuck," Niall spat out and stalked off.

"Strat," Connel said before he moved. "Your boy runs with Manzani… is that gonna be a problem?"

"Did. Past tense," Strat said. "He's got no love for Vex or his old man. My boy's straightened out."

Connel didn't give any clues on whether he believed that. "Wanna watch my woman? You're a McDade. You get that? Before anything else."

Strat looked at her. He hadn't asked for any of this and was being drawn back into a world he'd fought to free himself from.

"I get that," her friend said.

Her heart wept. She wanted so desperately to apologize, but sentiment wouldn't change anything. As he'd said, no one gave a shit about intentions.

"Get outta here," Connel said and Strat went.

Following orders. Because of her.

Tracking his progress, she kept on staring even after he'd disappeared down the stairs.

"He's got a thing for you."

She whipped around to Connel. "It's not like that," she said, tired of always having to justify herself. "I'm the same age as his daughter. He looks out for me."

"Yeah, he better. I'm paying him to keep you alive."

"Then cut me loose," she said, raising her arms as anger heated inside her. "Kick me out. Send me away. If I'm so damned inconvenient—"

"Control your anger." She'd said that to him and then they'd… "I don't have time now," he said like he read her mind. "The hit fucked my whole day and now this bullshit…"

"I'm sorry Daly got hurt."

"This is not only about you," he said, curling his fingers around a tendril of hair hanging over her cheek. "Our families have been enemies a long time."

Since they lost Dorsey, best she could figure. That wasn't the time for mysteries or work. Saving life and limb had to be the priority.

Would pleading dissuade him from confrontation?

The truth revealed another secret. "I don't want Evander to know it's you," she said. A frown creased his brow. "Send your guys. Don't go with them."

"Maybe it's why I'm fascinated," he muttered, confusing her. "You don't know integrity, loyalty—"

"Would you stop?" she snapped, smacking both hands on his chest to shove, though he didn't move. She caught the sheet before it fell from her breasts. "You say that like it's no big deal—"

"Loyalty is everything. Not having it… That's foreign to me."

"But it's not true," she said. "I love my family. I kept them out of the Manzani mess to protect them. I did this. I agreed to be yours to protect their livelihoods, their reputations."

"I send my soldiers out there to defend you and your reaction is shame? My family is everything, my people, my name, it's my birthright, my responsibility—"

"You think I'm ashamed? Of your family? Shit, Conn, I'm a complete fucking idiot around you! I'm ashamed of me! What kind of woman falls into bed with a guy as dangerous and powerful as you without expecting it to be a play? You record me, threaten to ruin me, and what do I do? Have a foursome with you!" Her throat narrowed; she couldn't breathe and talk at the same time and had to gasp for air. "I lose all sense around you. I lose every ounce of sanity, every inhibition… Every second we're together, all I want to do is drag you to bed… Fuck, I don't even care about bed, I'd probably do you anywhere! I'm so desperate to please you, to just be near you, and it doesn't make any fucking sense!" Gulping in another breath, all of her tingled with weakness that culminated in the sickness of butterflies dancing in her stomach. She couldn't look at him and face her humiliation so walked a dozen paces toward the window. "When I think about Evander touching me, from the second we met, it revolted me. He revolted me… I promised I'd never share myself with him. With you, I can't… I can't stop sharing… I can't stop wanting you…" Her head went back as she appealed to the heavens. "There's something wrong with me. I'm supposed to be smarter than this."

The glide of his fingertips down her upper arms was the first hint of his proximity.

"There are cameras in every room up here." Those fingertips sizzled against her, drawing lazy lines on her sensitive flesh. "I control them from my phone. They'll be on live feed… for my eyes only."

"Because Dasha is coming over?" she asked.

Was he asking her to put on a show?

"Whenever I'm not here, I'll be watching." The low rumble of that brogue obliterated whatever was left of her weak defenses. "No one touches you unless I'm in the room, no one without my express permission." As he spoke, he took control of the sheet, dropping it to the floor to cradle her breasts. "And we're gonna forget everything you just said. You give a guy like me that kind of power over you, he'll exploit it. I'll exploit it. I'm dangerous, remember?"

Her head fell back against him. "It tastes so good…" she breathed, her hand snaking around to his thigh. "If you were evil, you wouldn't warn me, you'd just exploit me." Cupping the bulge in his slacks, she squeezed and rubbed him through the frustrating material. "Conn…"

"Not that voice… Now you know what it does to me, you're exploiting it," he said, grabbing her shoulders to spin her around and scrutinize her face. "You know what happens if you play me."

If he got himself killed for pride, they wouldn't get that far.

"Stay here. With me," she said, sliding the leather from his belt buckle. "It's safe here."

"He doesn't get to touch you and come for my guys without consequences. No one does."

"If there's security, you could get hurt before you see him."

"We create a distraction," he said. "Get his guys out so we can break in."

Okay, that was a little reassuring.

"We could have sex," she said. "Somewhere he'll see. That would send a message." And he was safer in bed with her than anywhere near Evander. "Conn."

"I thought you didn't want him to know I'm your guy."

"Because I don't want him to hurt you," she said. "But I thought I lost that argument."

"You did."

"He's been watching me for years," she said. "Off and on. I don't think he'll react well to learning you were inside me less than twenty-four hours after we met." Which put a thought in her head. "You're not going to show him the footage, are you?"

"Because of our deal?"

"Because I don't want him to see me like that, to know me like that." When she tried to push away, he caught her in his embrace. "I don't want him to see me naked or to know—"

"You scream when you come?" he asked. "Or hear that sharp little inhale that escapes when I kiss you… or the satisfaction I get in the surrender when you sink against me?"

She didn't know she did any of that. Obviously, he did.

"I have to leave with Strat," she said.

"Why?"

"If I don't and Evander's people know I'm still in here…"

"We'll spread word you went out the back."

"Is there a back?"

"If you don't know, he doesn't. We need the element of surprise showing up at the hotel tonight."

With that, she could help. "Can I give you something?"

"I don't have time now—"

"Not something sexual," she said. He'd already declared his lack of disposable time yet was still there. "Something in my purse that might help you later."

He held her for another second but relented, and she scurried over to retrieve the plastic from her purse.

When she turned back, he was right there. "This," she said, holding it out to him. "Platinum Suite."

His intrigue became a scowl. "He gave you a key?"

"If you can create a distraction and his guys aren't on the floor, won't it be easier just to waltz in?"

"Says a lot," he said, turning it over in his hand. "Sends a message. He knows he gave you this… if I use it to get in his room…"

"There's only one person it could've come

from," she said. "I know. He'll think either you killed me or—"

"I'm your guy."

Their eyes met.

"I have no love for the Manzanis," she said, resting a hand on his chest. "I know what your family means to you. I don't take what you're doing for me for granted either."

"Don't leave this building."

"Will you come back here after?"

"Maybe."

She smiled. Never committing. Staying loose. He was protecting her; she couldn't ask for more. Shouldn't want it or even be thinking about it.

Maybe after their showdown, one of them would be down or gone. Everything was a mess, and it was all her fault.

NINE

"I DON'T SEE why we can't just—"

"Ire's rules," Dasha said. "Stop whining, Darla."

All night the blondes on the office chesterfield sniped at each other. One thing, then another. They weren't good at being idle. Was anyone? Working at his desk, she didn't make as good a view as Connel. Still, small mercies, at least they had their clothes on.

From memory, she was putting together a timeline and a list of questions in the notepad Dasha brought with the rest of the supplies earlier. Together, they'd written a list of needs and she'd stayed put while the beauties went shopping. Being a step removed was frustrating. The situation better damn well resolve itself soon or she'd be a prisoner in Stag for the rest of her days.

Strat sat at the end of the desk. Arms folded. Trapped in her vortex. Sucked into the foreverness that was Evander Manzani's obsession. Her friend definitely had better ways to spend his time.

"What time is it?" Darla asked.

She checked her phone. "Just after eleven."

"If we went down to the—"

"We can't!" Dasha asserted, bouncing on the couch. "We're not allowed."

Darla whined. "Why are we not allowed? If Ire doesn't need us—"

"It's Ser's rules," Dasha said. "Ire said we're to stay with her. She's in charge."

"He did?" she asked as her phone rang.

"Ire?" Dasha asked, perking up.

"No," she said, answering the phone, getting to her feet. "Hey."

"Hey," Lachlan said. "It's late. What you doing answering the phone this late?"

"You called me," she said, passing Strat to go through the curtain and up the stairs. "I always answer my phone. What if you have a hot tip for me?"

"Told you a million times, I won't be your source."

"Yeah, that's what Imogen's for," she said, curling her legs under her as she sat on the couch. "I can't complain. She sucked your dick for like three years. The woman's paid her dues. Poor thing."

"Thanks," he said. "Listen, when was the last time you heard anything about Vex?"

"Oh…" she said, drawing it out. "So you're not my source, but I'm yours? What's going on?"

"You have a strange fetish for him and his lifestyle."

"Trust me, you're way off base."

Though, glancing around, substituting one name for another, he wouldn't be so far from the mark.

"Can I take that to mean you haven't heard from him?"

Hiding anything from the brother she loved was difficult. It was easiest to tell the truth as much as possible.

"I spoke to him yesterday," she said. "Why?"

"You spoke to him? Are you fucking kidding me? Ser, why would you—"

"You want me to be honest with you?" she asked. "What happened to the 'I'll never get mad at the truth' rule we had when I was a kid?"

"You shouldn't be hanging out with guys like him." His voice was heavy. "You should know better by now."

"I wasn't hanging out with him. We… came across each other." Which only one of them had known would happen in advance. "You want me to lie? Say I haven't seen him?" And there was always the chance her brother was testing her. Could he know more than he was letting on? "Think whatever you want, Lach."

"No, I'm sorry," he said on an exhale. "There's a lot of… strain around here tonight."

"If you're calling me for information, you're desperate," she said. "He part of your case?"

"We got word he might be responsible for a shipment coming in tonight," he said, his volume low. "We have to intercept this one and—"

"Isn't that more narcotics gig?" she asked. "If they dropped the ball—"

"It's not a shipment of drugs," he said. "We thought it was, at first, from the chatter on—"

"If not drugs, what…" A prickle of trepidation trickled up her spine. "Women… you're talking about human trafficking." Knowing her brother's division, she should've got there sooner. "They're bringing women in, probably sending them off to brothels all over the city."

"And further," he said. "They use the city as a hub and unless we can intercept them before—"

"Evander didn't say anything about women. He wouldn't talk to me about something like that."

"No, I know, but… We're watching his club. 'Cept we just found out he's not here. If he wants to be there while the women are coming in—"

"You want to know where he is," she whispered, glancing toward the bedroom.

"Like I said, with your weird fetish—you've done a lot of research on the family. And although you won't reveal them, you have sources who might know…"

Licking her lips, she needed more time. Except if the cops descended when Connel was there…

She squeezed her eyes closed. "He's at the Grand… Platinum Suite."

"How the fuck do you know that?"

"You don't want to know."

"Why not?"

"You're my brother."

"Oh, God, Ser, please don't tell me you're …"

"There? No," she said. "But you better be quick if you don't want to test that."

"Shit," he said. "Okay. We are not done talking about this."

He hung up. Damnit. What had she just done?

Pouncing off the couch, she ran back to the office. The blondes. Right.

"You want to go downstairs?" she asked them, aiming for breezy.

"Da!" Darla exclaimed. "I need to dance!"

"You should," she said, smiling. "You totally should. Both of you."

"Really?" Dasha asked, hesitant although she stood. "Ire said we should stay with you."

"I'm fine. Go. Have fun."

Darla grabbed Dasha and, ignoring the latter's reluctance, ran from the room.

The second they were gone, Strat was on his feet. "What's going on?"

Her cheer cleared in a panicked instant. "Have you got Connel's number?"

"No, Niall's."

"Good," she said, struck by relief. "The cops are on their way to the hotel."

"Shit," he said, scrambling for his phone. "What did you do?"

Good question. Who the hell knew? "Should we leave?"

"Don't think we want to fight our way out," he said, dialing and raising the phone to his ear.

He turned his back as he spoke.

Connel may never speak to her ever again. If he did, she would get his number. Having information and no way to get it to him was too terrifying an experience to repeat.

Strat turned to her, his expression stony.

"What did he say?"

"You're to stay put," he said. "Upstairs."

And she doubted the blondes would be joining them in bed.

Upstairs.

Did he want them alone or to cut off her escape routes?

TEN

SHE DIDN'T WANT to sleep but couldn't sit still. Strat was on a stool, back to the bar, twisting left to right, following her progress, pacing up and down the living room.

Hundreds of people on the floor below danced their time away without a care in the world. Damn did she envy them.

She'd thought getting the info was difficult. That telling Lachlan was stressful. Those were nothing to how she worried in the silence.

Until Connel walked in, until she laid eyes on him, she wouldn't relax. Anything could happen. What if Lachlan got there quickly? Had the McDade posse been in the hotel already? She didn't want them arrested on her tip.

A door slammed and she stopped, fixated on the stairs.

Connel came jogging into view.

Without even looking at her, he strode across the room. "Out," he said to Strat as he rounded the bar.

Strat looked at her as he rose. If she asked him to stay, he would. With a slight nod, she gave him the silent go. Connel was pissed. No doubt. He might kick her out, but he wouldn't hurt her.

Her bodyguard disappeared down the stairs.

Connel slammed a glass on the counter and poured out some liquor.

"You're pissed," she said, going to the bar. "I'm sorry. I didn't mean to tell him. He called and was trying to find—this was about saving lives." He drank. "Evander's bringing women into the city. Trafficking women. He's the cop's only hope of finding them. They have to question him, to save these women. To free them, the cops have to find them."

The glass hit the bar again. Hard. His eyes tapered, their depth darkening, zeroing in on her.

His hand disappeared into his inside pocket and then a cellphone was at his ear. "Manzani's Russian dolls, where are they?" He paused, hung up, and dropped the phone by his drink. "Amber Corner, Rector Base, third floor."

Damn. How had he…? Maybe she should've thought about asking him.

"Just like that you can…" On an exhale, she got it. "You know things."

"I know things," he said and drank the last of the liquor.

After slamming the glass down, he came around to snatch her wrist and dragged her to the bedroom. He swung her around, throwing her down on the bed.

In her recovery, sweeping her hair from her face, he whipped his belt from its loops to snap it loud. The sound cracked in her gut, hollowing her out to make way for need.

"Is this how we argue?" she asked, rising on her knees.

"No arguing. We have a deal. You do what you're told," he said, throwing the belt aside to unbutton his shirt. "Lose it."

"What?"

"Everything."

Moisture rushed her throat; need overtook caution. Do as she was told. That was the deal, and, fuck, if she didn't love being reminded. Unzipping, she lost her dress and bra as she walked down the bed on her knees.

This wasn't like any other fight with a partner. Usually, she'd expect yelling. Anger. Sneers, insults, and backbiting. Where was the fear? The regret? Resentment, contrition, none of her emotions were negative, despite him vibrating with disapproval.

He jerked his shirt off his shoulders one at a time to throw it aside while she worked on his pants. The moment they were loose, he grabbed her jaw to haul her attention up.

"You are a subordinate, you exist beneath me, under me," he growled. "Don't think. Don't make decisions. Your life is mine. You are mine. McDade property on my terms. My limits. You obey. Yield. Surrender. You don't resist. You don't get in my way. Your job is to support me. Say it."

He loosened his grip just enough to let her speak. "My job is to support you."

His ace? The video. The tool trapping her in his bed. Or was it? The recording didn't explain why her hand slipped into his pants of its own freewill. Already full, his cock wanted to play, even if the ferocity burning from his gaze said otherwise.

Balling his fist in her hair, he bowed to get in her face. "Suck it," he said, releasing her jaw, forcing her head down.

That was it. The order she'd anticipated. As a sharp spasm of excitement burst through her pussy, her hungry mouth sought his dick.

She hadn't meant to disobey or embarrass him. His approval meant something. He'd been out there, in part, defending her, and she'd ruined his plan in the most intrusive way.

Shit, she wanted to please him. Wanted to apologize with the physical he understood. Except he didn't fit in her throat, simple as that. She tried and failed. Tried and failed. Sucking and licking, working her hand up and down his shaft, she tried desperately to satisfy him. Peeking up, the elevated angle of his chin hid his expression. Did he want her? Enjoy her efforts? His pelvis moved, pushing himself deeper as his constricted hand forced her closer.

On his first real thrust, she gagged. He didn't slow or stop; it was on her to breathe. To learn him, to find the rhythm. The sting of his tightened fingers in her hair shot all the way to her temples. Fuck, it felt good. He felt good. The speed, how his first hand joined the second and his pace picked up.

On a curse, he pulled her away, freeing her mouth to flip her onto her back. He dropped to his knees and, with one tug, brought her head off the edge of the bed. She'd never performed for a guy that way before, upside down. He ran the head of his dick across her lips, coating her in the need seeping from him.

"Open," he snarled, grabbing her breast when her jaw loosened.

Feeding her his cock, he pushed, hard, fast, right into her throat. It was panic, no breath, pain, then… that fullness slipped away and she immediately wanted it back. He granted her wish and drove into her, his thrusts quick but deep. Every time he pushed in to the hilt, his balls squashed against her, blocking her nose. Breathing needed to match the tempo, which she only just got a moment before he fired into her, shooting his desire so deep, she almost choked when he withdrew.

Her labored breathing slowed but stayed intense. He'd just… they'd just…

What the fuck was that?

"Good girl," he murmured as he rose to go into the bathroom.

Her pussy tingled, and she lay there, looking into the bedroom, upside down, focused on nothing.

Running her hands across her breasts, she closed her eyes, considering whether she should touch herself or hope he'd come back to finish the job.

"Up." When she opened her eyes and raised her head, he was standing by the side of the bed. "Up."

"We're done?" she asked, struggling to sit.

"Go wash up."

At something of a loss, she went to get ready for bed, brushing her teeth and washing her face.

In the closet, she checked through the clothes Dasha bought. "Dasha didn't bring me anything to sleep in," she said, peeking into the bedroom. "Can I borrow a shirt?"

He was already lying down, the sheet draped across his hips. "No. You sleep naked in my bed."

Okay, or that was an option. Was Dasha under specific instructions to accommodate that wish?

Switching off the closet light, she went to the bed, skimming a leg across him to straddle his hips. "Still pissed?" she asked, opening her hands on his stomach.

"Cops will have him all weekend," he said, his fingers locked behind his head, eyes fixed on the ceiling. "I won't get near him until next week."

That was a yes. Still pissed.

"Do you understand why I told Lachlan?"

"No, I don't," he said. "You have a problem? You bring it to me. That's my job. To fix it."

"I don't have your number," she said, stroking

him. "Which reminds me…"

When she raised a leg, intending to climb off him, he caught her knee to push it back down. "I didn't give you permission to leave."

"My phone is downstairs," she said. "I need it."

"Why?"

"I want to put your number in it, and because my brother's going to call. My brother's a cop, remember? If I don't pick up, he'll have his guys ping my phone and come find me. He already thinks I'm sleeping with Evander. Can you imagine how he'd feel when this address came up?"

"Go get my phone."

Uh, okay… Being naked, tiptoeing across the living room to get his phone from the bar was a little nerve-wracking. If she was out there anyway, she could just hurry down the stairs to grab hers, but she was already on thin ice and didn't want to push him by taking initiative.

She took his device back to the bedroom, putting it in his hand as she climbed over him to her side of the bed.

"Why do you need it?" she asked, but he was already on a call.

"Bluebell's phone is in the office," he said into his. "Put the secondary number in and chip it. And get someone to tip—yeah."

He hung up and tossed the phone to his nightstand before putting his hands behind his head again.

"My phone needs to be chipped?" she asked, on her side, admiring his profile. "What does that mean?"

"Makes it untraceable," he said. "By outside agencies."

"Outside?"

"I'll still be able to find you."

"That's fine. I'm used to abandoning my phone when I want to go off radar anyway. My dad started tracking me long before Evander did."

His jaw twitched. "Don't say his name."

"Were you at the hotel? Did he know you were there?"

"No," he said. "He'll know your brother was though."

"So he'll be pissed at me," she said, curling her arm beneath the pillow. That was going to happen either way. "Saved him learning about us. I don't blame you if you want to wash your hands of me."

"He'll have bigger things to worry about when they cut him loose."

"He will? Like what?"

"That shipment was his," he said. "Not part of his father's agenda."

"Oh," she said, wriggling closer. "That's a bonehead move. His father is the head of the family. Silvio is not a guy anyone should mess with."

"Have you met him?"

"Silvio? No, not in the flesh," she said, smiling when his hand left his head to seek hers. He didn't look at her, just took her hand to flatten it on his chest, his heavy on top. "We write sometimes."

"Write?" he asked, adjusting his head to meet her eye. "You write to Silvio Manzani?"

"He wasn't a fan of my article."

"He threatened you?"

"He's too smart for that," she said, opening her fingers so his could sink between them. "I wrote to Helios too; we've had a back and forth for a while." Few people knew about her connection to Vex's incarcerated older brother, Helios "Hell" Manzani. And, yes, if the stories were true, he lived up to the title. "Didn't Silvio Manzani and your dad used to be close?"

"The families were allies back in those days," he said, his focus returning to the ceiling. "United against others. Silvio was closer to my uncle."

"Your uncle worked under your father in the Midwest operation."

Another head shift. This time he was frowning. "And?"

"Burl ran things on the east coast, right? You had to strengthen ties there yourself after… everything." His frown deepened. "Do you still talk to Burl?"

"Planning another article?"

"Sort of," she said. Before he could shift away, she rested her chin on his chest. "It would give us cover."

"Cover?"

"For being around each other. If anyone asks questions, I can tell them I'm writing a story on the McDades."

"Anyone asks questions, you call me."

Except she wouldn't do that with her family and Steeple.

"Steeple will worry about me," she said. "He checks in with his people and wanted me to write a follow up on the Manzani exposé. If I'm going to miss meetings and be off the grid, I have to give him a reason for shadowing you or he'll worry."

"Print one word about me, my family, or my operations, he'll have reason to worry."

Although that was a poorly veiled threat, she slid a leg across him to straddle him again. This time, she bowed to join their lips for a brief kiss.

"Trust… Aren't we building that?"

"McDades have been in the press enough."

"The trial," she murmured, kissing him. "Burl's conviction, Biz's—"

Grabbing her upper arms, he flipped them over, putting himself on top. "Think you can fuck with me?

Think I'll fall for that shit? Betray me and I won't hesitate to open your pretty throat ear to ear."

"I was worried about you," she confessed, relaxing even as his grip tightened and his glare darkened. "Even after you knew the cops were on their way, I was scared you'd be caught up in it."

"You could've let us walk into that. Got all of us in one net."

Which hadn't occurred to her for a second. "I don't want the cops to have you," she said, raising her head to seek his lips, though he jerked out of the way. "I can't go twenty-five to life without feeling you inside me… Conn…"

"Fuck," he hissed, his mouth swooping down onto hers.

Raising her arms, he pinned them above her head, holding her down as his tongue plunged deeper.

What was she doing? This wasn't smart. Her honesty with him… Her feelings. He had every reason not to trust her. Yet he'd shared privileged information. If she revealed that to her brother or her father, to anyone else, Connel McDade would be in serious trouble.

Still, it wasn't tempting. He had the tape, the ability to ruin her. Leverage. Tit for tat. Everything about them and their lives contrasted, but as his hand insinuated itself between them to play with her pussy, she was ready to give him anything he wanted.

ELEVEN

LATER, LAZING on top of him in their sex sheets, time slowed.

"It's like a game," she said.

"What's a game?"

"This," she said, stroking his arm. "I have this to leverage, you have that… back and forth…"

"It's how the world works."

She laughed. "No, it isn't."

"Everything is barter. We do what benefits number one."

"Going after Evander tonight wasn't looking after number one," she said. "You could've been hurt or killed. And don't you always say your loyalty is to your family before anything else?"

"The family is my number one."

"With Burl and Biz in prison, your dad dead, the McDades are falling fast," she said. "Do you still speak with Score, Play, and Razer?"

"Aye."

"And you took over everything Doherty that

didn't go down with the ship. Your families are connected now."

"I have boots on the ground and a hand on the wheel. Whisper's head of her family."

Not that there was much of it left.

"Easy to do, I guess, with a McDade like Razer at her back. What's she like?" she asked, sitting up on him. "I've heard some incredible things about Whisper Doherty. Did she really murder a woman for smiling at her husband?"

"Almost," he said, running his palms up her torso, over her breasts and back down. "She's possessive."

"It's incredible." Her hands rested on his, moving with his as they caressed her. "Two combative families, both such extreme personalities… it's a wonder their marriage has lasted this long."

"She's possessive, sure, but McDades have a jealous streak. Raze has put bullets in men for looking at his wife. Crippled them for touching her. She plays to it. Woman's fierce."

"Not all McDades," she said, her hips undulating as his cock awoke beneath her.

"Not all McDades, what?"

"Have a jealous streak." Or Connel just didn't care about her enough to get jealous. "You don't."

"Don't test that theory, baby," he said, squeezing her breasts together.

Resting her hands on his torso, she lifted and dropped just a few inches, mimicking what they'd done twice already.

"We had sex with two other people," she said. "You weren't jealous then."

"No?"

"Is that what you want? You want your other girls here? They're dancing in the club."

If the club was still open, time meant nothing in that room.

"You need them?"

"No," she said, rocking against him. "Even when I was with them, all I thought about was how bad I needed you inside me."

"They're your extras, babe. Not mine."

"You've been with both of them in the past, haven't you?"

"Yeah," he said, tormenting her nipples with his thumbs. "Been with a lot of women."

Given who he was, that was no surprise.

"You just have to pick and point, don't you?"

"Aye," he said and sat up, wrapping both arms around her to hold her close. "I can give you any woman you want."

Because he'd already said men weren't allowed near her.

"I wasn't thinking that," she said, parting her lips when his teased without making contact. "You torture me."

"I could do that," he breathed. "You want pain, baby?"

"This is pain… wanting you so much."

Especially while his solid cock pressed against her pussy. Her hips reacted, writhing and wriggling, stimulating her hormones, igniting her endorphins.

"Tastes good, doesn't it?"

"So good," she groaned.

His sly pleasure shivered through her. "Doing something wrong feels good."

"Feels dirty."

"Because it's naughty," he taunted, squeezing her ass in both hands, pushing up against her. "I'm a bad guy… and you're supposed to be a good girl. Why you want a guy like me, naughty girl?"

Clenching her inner muscles, she could feel her wetness surge. "Naughty?"

"Mm," he said, kissing her once before whispering against her, "so naughty. You're a naughty girl."

"Don't naughty girls get punished?"

His grip stayed tight, but he leaned back, assessing her. "You want me to punish you?"

"Yeah," she panted. "You want me to be a good girl?"

"I like you dirty," he said, vaulting off the bed, her still in his embrace. "Even dirty girls need to be taught."

She'd been nervous crossing the living room without clothes, but he didn't think twice about going downstairs without a stitch on either of them.

Strat could be in the office. Niall. Anyone. And they were just—

He didn't go through the curtain to the office. He rounded in a U-turn to open the mysterious door adjacent to the bottom of the stairs. Blue and pink lights flickered on in the new room, bathing everything in a purple hue.

He put her on her feet.

Where were they? What was…?

What she saw was… Huh, an intriguing space.

Bigger than she'd have thought, the room was lined in black leather, literally. All except for a flare of red leather on a closed door to the left. Tiered seating curved around the far wall, facing a central platform. The stage held a frame with chains running through eyebolts. Winches, padlocks, cuffs, ropes. In the center a padded leather bench, no, like a pommel horse, with its own cuffs and chains.

"Oh my God," she said, walking a few steps before spinning around to address him.

The wall behind him distracted her. Racks of toys. Strap-ons, paddles, vibrators, beads, plugs, ropes, and a row of open boxes filled with all kinds of condoms.

"Interested?"

"Geez, do you get these wholesale?" she asked, going past him to touch the edge of the leather covered box. Twirling, she leaned back against the bar at her back, smiling at him admiring her. "Guess the stories are true…"

"Always with the stories," he said. "Wanna try it?"

She glanced at the toys and ran her fingertips along a crop. "Play with the guy with no rules," she said, taking the crop from the rack, running it through her fingers as she returned to him. "Why not?"

"There are rules in this room," he said, taking the crop and her hand to lead her over to the platform.

"Is the door locked?"

"That's up to me." Guiding her to the end of the bench, he used his body to press her against it. Bending to push her head out of the way with his, he traced his lips across the pressure point above her clavicle. "My favorite nook," he breathed. Though she dammed her lips, a mew of arousal rolled in her throat. "That's it, purr for me, baby."

"Conn…"

"Try to manipulate me with that and I'll gag you," he said, thrusting his hips against her when hers pushed back. "Hands behind your back." When she followed orders, something warm and soft coiled around her wrists. "Now the rules… I am only master or sir while we play."

Heat pulsed downward. Already swollen and wet, she wanted speed. "Yes, sir," she said, subduing a laugh. He yanked, and leather bindings tightened around her wrists. Painfully tight. And when she tried to fight them, there was no give. "Conn—"

"Not so funny now," he said, hooking her hair back over her shoulder. "Sir or master."

"Sir," she said as he ran his fingertips from the back of her neck down to her ass. The tickle caught her breath, slinking up her spine to shimmer through her scalp. "Oh…"

It was difficult not to make sounds when he indulged her with those slight touches that rocked the floor beneath her feet. And that was before the pressure of his body left hers and his tongue touched the groove at the top of her ass to slither up with a feather's pressure, so lazy and scintillating that her breathing dropped, slowing to match his pace.

He got all the way to the nape of her neck. With a kiss, he exhaled, and a shiver crossed her shoulders.

"Relax," he whispered against her as his hands slid onto her shoulders, easing her forward, bending her over the horse.

The cool leather roused her nipples. "Yes, sir," she said because it felt good.

She frowned when he grabbed her ankle, picking her leg up to clamp metal around it.

"Next rule, everything I say goes. You take orders and don't question me."

After locking one ankle in place, he did the same to the second. Only him, the metal, and the horse held her up. The very tips of her toes were the only part of her that made contact with the floor.

"Conn—"

He thwacked her ass with the crop. The sudden biting pain dislodged a yelp from her throat.

"Sir." She almost said his name again, but… fixating on that buzz, on the tingle of discomfort it was… she laughed. "Do it again!"

"No," he said, running the end of the crop across

her ass and up her body as he walked around the horse. "Safe word first."

"I want this. I want to do this with you. I have never been so crazy with a guy, never—"

"Safe word," he said.

The stalk of the crop made harsh contact with both ass cheeks.

Okay, that was worse. She hissed through her teeth, closing her eyes to the sting. Stop. Pause. Neither of those worked. They needed a safe word neither of them would ever say in the casual—or not so casual—union of their bodies.

"I can't think of anything." Tossing her hair as best she could, she turned her head over to seek him out. Except, mmm, she was pretty much eye to eye with his cock. His naked, very interested in proceedings, cock. "Come closer."

Her hair fell over her eyes repeatedly; she kept trying to toss it out of the way. Her playmate didn't come any closer but stroked her hair away from her face with the end of the crop. Except he wasn't looking at her eager expression. His focus slunk up and down her body, absorbing her prone position, his power over her.

A whole new kind of pain took over. Like withdrawal, her stomach cramped, and she whined, desperate to reach out and sate her addiction.

"Dingo," she said when it leaped to mind. His attention found hers. "Isn't he the one who interrupted our first night?"

A straight yet satisfied slant to his lips inspired such freedom. Stepping forward, he pressed the head of his cock to her mouth.

Though she opened wide, he only drew it around her lips. "You're hungry."

Distracted by attempts to catch him in her mouth, she missed the movement of his arm. Three short, hard strokes changed that. They tensed her, clenching her muscles. What did it say about her that the sting of his punishment firing through her was so enlivening?

"Don't you worry, baby," he said, pushing himself into her throat. "I'm gonna take good care of you." Sucking on him, she sought his eyes as he undulated within her. "Want me to try the paddle? Gag that mouth? Fuck you 'til my balls are empty." He pulled out. "Answer me."

"Yes, sir," she said, sucking in her saliva to swallow.

"And when we're done," he said, tossing the crop aside to stroll around her.

With her ankles locked, she feared pushing too far either way in case she fell from the bench. But she wanted to see him, to know where he'd gone. She closed her eyes when he caressed her ass, stroking her with a delicate touch he wasn't known for. When his lips touched her butt, right at the sorest point, she smiled.

"Sir," she said on an exhale.

"I'm gonna take care of you," he said, still smoothing his rough fingers across her flesh. "Real good care of you."

TWELVE

THEIR PLEASURE DIDN'T end in that playroom. It didn't end that night. It kept going, hour after hour, day after day. Right there in Stag, in their own private bubble, occupied by them and no one else.

"C—Conn—Connel!" she screamed for him, her whole body locked in an arch, every muscle strained, frozen in orgasmic pleasure.

Pounding on the office door shattered the passion too soon.

"Boss!" someone shouted through the door. No, not someone, Niall. "Ire!"

"Shit," Connel barked, slamming a hand to the floor. "How many fucking times…!"

Laying her hands on his shoulders, they moved to soothe him as he sat up.

"Control," she whispered.

"What?" he snapped at the door. So much for control. "What the fuck do you want? We're busy!"

"Got the worm," Niall said.

Connel pounced to his feet, pulling off the

condom. "Two minutes," he said and disappeared through the curtain to go upstairs.

She was happy to stay there on the rug in the middle of his office.

The locked door Niall was behind had been that way for days. Locked. Two or three at least. She didn't know and couldn't care. They had everything they needed. Bed. Booze. The playroom. He'd told her pleasure would be the only rule and fuck, she wasn't sure how much more she could take... although...

Her palms grazed her nipples, rasping the sensitive, tortured peaks. They'd been pampered and spoiled by him, the man who'd taught her about pleasure in so many wonderful ways.

Something landed on her face. Fabric.

"Put that on," Connel said as she sat up to untwine the apparel. Though he only wore boxer-briefs, the barrier was disappointing. "You don't cover that body, I'll be inside it again, witnesses or not."

Even his casual comments aroused her. She put her arms in the sleeves and closed the material over her body before he opened the door.

Niall tried to step in, but Connel blocked him with an arm on the doorframe. Surprise registered on Niall's expression when it landed on her.

She opened a hand in a wave, still holding the two sides of her shirt in one fist.

"What is it?" Connel demanded of his number two.

"Club's opening," Niall said. "We've got an eyeball on him."

"The club's opening? Stag?" she asked, processing his words. "Is it Monday?"

"Aye," Niall said.

She scrambled to her feet. "Damnit."

"Stay there," Connel said, using the closure of

the door to push his underling out. "Where d'you think you're going?"

When she went to him and laid a hand on his torso, she boosted onto her tiptoes for a kiss, but he didn't come down to meet her.

"Baby, I got away with not talking to Lachlan this weekend because I agreed to dinner with him tonight."

"I want you here."

"Are you staying here?" she asked.

Niall showing up with news often led to Connel being imminently busy.

"Strat will drive you."

"What will Lach say to that?"

"Sell him the story line," he said, ducking to kiss her. "Your genius plan."

That he hadn't been wild about when she mentioned it. "So I can say it's your car, your driver…" her smile got playful yet saucy, "that I'm studying you?"

Rather than another kiss, he grabbed her to spin her around and pin her to the door. His head rested on hers and he growled before crouching to hook her thighs and pick her up.

"I want you back here within the hour," he said as her legs coiled around him.

"Dinner takes more than an hour," she said, her words becoming breathy when his lips explored her throat and her fingers tangled in his hair. "Conn… baby…"

He boosted her higher, burying his face in her cleavage. "Should tie you down," he mumbled.

Niall might be right on the other side of the door. She didn't care. They'd done it everywhere else, the desk, the couch, the rug.

"I need your cock," she groaned on an exhale, grinding against his hard body as he rubbed his rough stubble against her sensitive breasts.

"You've got me hooked," he growled, kissing her nipple then dragging his teeth against her. "Fucking addicted."

"Conn…" she gasped when he sucked so hard, she could feel a bruise form. "Sink into me."

"Fucking cheap crack whore."

Curling her fingers, she tugged hard on his hair. "Hey!" she said, smiling at his drowsy eyes. "What did you call me?"

In his defense, he looked high. Maybe she did too.

"Me, baby," he said, letting her slide down so he could kiss her lips. "I'm the crack whore."

"And I'm the crack?" she asked, laughing as she sought his kiss. "You have been easy all weekend, whoring yourself with me."

"You taught me easy, baby," he said, turning so fast, she had to loop her arms around him to steady herself.

"We're not going out?"

"You want to go to your brother covered in me?" he asked, carrying her up the stairs. "I don't mind sending McLeod a message."

"Send this McLeod a message," she said, nuzzling his neck. "Sink into me, McDade…" Her fingers kept combing into his hair as she spoiled him with short kisses. "My McDade."

He took them into the shower and turned on the water before putting her on her feet.

"Wait here."

When he tried to leave, she caught his wrist. "Shower with me."

"We need another rubber."

Thank God he got them wholesale. He left her there, slipping off his underwear as he went. She shirked the shirt and tossed it over the top of the screen.

More rubbers. More sex. Would it ever be enough?

THIRTEEN

"IT'S NOT THAT BAD," she said, stabbing a chunk of salmon with her fork. "Stop circling back to it."

"You know I spent all weekend interrogating that asshole," Lachlan said, putting down his beer. "You know, the last one you obsessed about."

"I wasn't obsessed with Evander—"

"You want to tell me now how you knew where Manzani was?"

"No," she said, adjusting the napkin in her lap.

She could feel him, like he was still inside her. Connel. Bruised and spent, he'd pampered her pussy all weekend. He wasn't even there. She didn't know where he was, but she could feel him all over her body. In every crevice and corner he'd indulged.

"Just no?" her brother asked. "You wouldn't have known where he was if he didn't invite you. There's a reason two people meet in a hotel."

"Really?" she asked, feigning innocence. "What's the reason, Lach?"

His head relaxed to the side. "Play with me, that's

funny. 'Til he knocks you up."

"I can promise Evander will never have that privilege. And not that it's your business, but I have an IUD, brother."

Concern smacked him. "This is the guy who abducts women and chains them to beds for anyone and everyone to screw. I don't care how into him you are, use protection. Shit, I'll get you a doc appointment myself. God knows what he gave you."

"Usually Dad takes the job of demeaning me. Are you following suit?"

"I'm sorry," he said. "I'm your brother, I worry about you. Sue me."

"You don't have to worry. I'm safe and sane."

"I thought that until you told me about your new McDade story. Don't you want to lie low? You can't have a Manzani and a McDade in your life. That guarantees disaster."

Her brother accepted her explanation for the car and the driver, for her following around another gangster. Well, accepted was a strong word. This lecture had been going on since they sat down and ordered. Thank God they'd foregone appetizers. Already it felt like they'd been there for days.

"From what you've said about Evander," she said, "he has bigger things to worry about."

"We couldn't tie him to the women. We know it was him, but not from any source that would stand up in court."

"How did you find them?" she asked, twisting her fork in the tagliatelle. "The women?"

"Anonymous tip. Someone got word from an informant."

"That was lucky."

An anonymous tip. Could it be an anonymous McDade source? Connel wouldn't mind screwing with

Manzani, there was no loyalty there. She'd have to ask.

"For those women, sure. Some of them were in a bad state."

"What will happen to them now?"

"Everyone got medical attention. Some will be sent back, some will stay."

"Bet they were glad to see you."

"Unlike Manzani," he said. "The way he'd set up that hotel room…" he exhaled and pushed his plate aside. "Are you in trouble?"

"No," she said, enjoying her food, maybe because she hadn't eaten much the last three days and had to replenish her stores. "Why would you think I was in trouble?"

"You were talking about doing something you didn't want to do last week. Then you know where Vex is and tell me you're writing an article about McDade. Is he how you knew Vex's location?" No, it was the other way around. "If you're mixed up in something and need help, I'm always here for you."

"I know that." She smiled. "I do and I'm fine."

His phone rang. "Sorry," he said, retrieving it from his pocket.

It was nice of him to apologize, but in his profession, sometimes unexpected things cropped up. Kind of like Connel's life too.

"McLeod," he answered the call. She poured more wine into her glass to drink. "When…? No, I'm on my way." He hung up. "I'm sorry, sis, something's happened. I have to take you home."

"What happened?" she asked as he took out his wallet.

"Vex just landed at the hospital."

"Vex? Evander?" she asked, infused by shock. "What happened?"

"That's what I'm gonna find out."

She pushed out her chair and grabbed her purse. "I'm coming with you."

"What? No, you're not. No."

She smiled and stood when he did. "Unfortunately, you can't stop me. It's a free country." She slid the strap of her purse up to her shoulder. "And I have a car on the curb with a driver." Who had kept a low profile so as not to be seen. "Do you have a car on the curb?" No, he didn't, but that didn't seem to sway him. Her smug smile stretched. "Who do you think Evander's more likely to see?"

That got his attention. He sighed. "Fine. Come on."

FOURTEEN

LACHLAN KNEW HIS way around the emergency room. Knew plenty of the staff too. The females especially. Her brother was cute, in a brother type way, but it was always a little strange to see how many women swooned when he showed up.

A nurse led the way for them.

"This way," Lachlan said, catching her shoulder to guide her after the nurse. "He got beat up. Broke a couple of ribs. Got stabbed too."

"Stabbed?" she asked and stopped to look at her brother. Shit, that was a big one. Why not lead with that? "By whom?" Some part of her was already answering that question. "Oh my God."

"He hasn't said by who," he said, getting her moving again. "Guys like that don't. Won't. We'll find out when someone shows up in the morgue tomorrow. Going after a Manzani kid like this, it's insane. Silvio will pull out all the stops."

"Maybe," she said as they paused outside the room.

"Wait here," the nurse said and went in.

"Maybe?" he asked, getting closer. "What is maybe? I thought you knew how these families worked. They can't let this assault stand or it weakens them."

"It's about pride," she said, restraining an eye roll. "I know." She shrugged. "We just don't know what's going on in the family, do we? How do you know one of his wasn't responsible for it?"

The nurse poked her head out the door. "He'll see Sersha, he won't see you, Lach."

She was about to step forward, but Lachlan held her back. "He sees both of us or neither of us."

Having provoked her brother into accompanying her with that tactic, she couldn't argue with him for calling her on it.

"Princess!" Evander hollered.

The nurse stepped aside to let her into the private room. Had he been such a nightmare they had to separate him, or was this hospitality reserved for Manzanis?

"Princess," he said, reaching out to her.

Even she had to stop. Plenty of times she'd wished Evander out of her life and thought he deserved to be taught a lesson. But with his bruised eye, the blood matted in his hair, the swollen lip… Shit. And that was just what she could see.

When he elevated the top of the bed to sit up, the discoloration on his neck sped her heart.

"Come over here, Princess," he said, holding his hand out to her.

Blood on the sheets and his knuckles… If Connel was responsible… What the hell was she doing there?

"Had some trouble, Manzani?" Lachlan said, passing her to go closer to the bed. "Wow, looks like you pissed someone off."

"I wanna see my Princess," Evander said, glaring. "I got nothing for you."

"Didn't think so," Lachlan said, folding his arms. "Want to make a report?" Evander didn't care about the cop; his focus remained on her. "Yo! Manzani!"

"Don't shout," she said, putting one foot in front of the other to get to the bedside. "Did someone call your father?"

"I'm sure he's heard," Evander said, relaxing though he raised his hand toward hers.

She didn't want to hold his hand. If this was Connel and Vex said something… her brother was behind her… not a good combination.

Putting her hand in Evander's, she bit her tongue and played nice.

"You want justice?" Lachlan said. "You've got to tell us who's responsible. Where were you at tonight?"

"Taking care of business," Evander said. "Had some delays this weekend."

Yeah, because he'd been with the cops.

"That cause trouble?" her brother asked. "I could've helped you out there too."

"You're a lucky guy," Evander said, yanking her closer. She stumbled a step, and her brother caught her, but Evander got close enough to whisper in her ear. "He'll pay for touching you."

"Hands off, Manzani," Lachlan said, jerking her away to put her behind him. "Want me to pull you in for assault?"

"Maybe you should. Take a good look. Imagine what the other guy looks like."

She had to get back. Had to see him. Without even thinking, she walked away from Lachlan, out of the room, and down the corridor.

"Ser!" Lachlan called after her. "Sersha!" She got all the way to the door before he caught up and grabbed her arm. "Hey… what's wrong? Did he say something?"

"No," she said, fighting to compose herself. "No, I just… didn't expect him to look like that."

"It's okay," he said, giving her a hug. "This is why I didn't want you to come."

"Sorry, I—"

"I'll take you home."

Home wasn't where she wanted to go. Strat was driving, but she'd told him to stay in the car no matter what. He had to. If Lachlan saw him, it would raise too many questions. They didn't exactly have the best relationship with each other. That was between them, nothing to do with her. Well, them and the woman between them, Strat's daughter.

Lachlan urged her into the car and got in behind her. She had no choice and had to follow. Lachlan would put her in her apartment; he always did after dark. He'd put her inside and get a cab. She'd have to text Strat and let him know what was going on. He might leave when Lachlan took her inside, but she'd need him to loop back when her brother was gone.

With Lachlan in the back seat at her side, she couldn't call Connel, but she had to see him. To know he was okay, to know what happened. Except if he wasn't at the club… where else could she look?

****

LACHLAN TOOK IT upon himself to check her apartment for intruders, not that she expected any.

He gave the big brother speech about the dangers of bad boys too. Little did he know she was rushing him out just to get back to hers.

After he left, it seemed to take Strat an age to return. Wherever he'd gone, he hadn't understood her urgency.

"Where were you?" she asked, getting in the front. "I almost got a cab."

"Figured you'd need the time to calm down," Strat said. "Cool off. Guess that brother of yours didn't talk any sense into you."

"Have you heard?"

"That Manzani junior is laid up? Yeah. I took you to the hospital."

"No," she said. "From Conn?"

"We don't keep in touch."

"From Niall, from anyone. Geez, Strat, what's wrong with you?"

"What's wrong with me? What's wrong with you? Yeah, I got the call about Vex from like five guys before your cop got a clue. It's serious shit, Ser. Serious. I wouldn't let my Immie be anywhere near this kinda crap. What's wrong with you? You should run a mile."

Maybe he was right. "Weren't you the one who said I needed a bad boy?"

"No, I said they turned you on. Given what you and the boss spent the weekend doing, I think we know I'm right. But when does sense kick in? You're lucky, damn lucky, McDade didn't kill him. I'm fucking shocked he didn't. Never heard of him being light on the trigger... Did you talk to him? Ask him not to take Manzani out?"

"You think he'd listen if I did?"

"We don't know what goes on behind closed doors... The guys were... McDade's never done it, locked the door on him and a woman. Niall grew up at his side. The boss has never had a singular focus like he does with you."

"He doesn't have a singular focus," she said. Though three days and nights beneath him probably suggested otherwise to his men. "I didn't know he was going after Evander tonight." Though she'd suspected he could be the worm Niall referenced. "He didn't tell me and I didn't ask."

"You've got the moll thing down already," he said and flashed her a smile. "I get on your case because I care about you."

"I know."

"My little girl doesn't listen to me either, I'm used to it."

"I know," she said and sighed. "But Imogen doesn't put you in the line of fire. I'm sorry you ended up in this, watching my ass. I know you didn't want this."

"It was my choice," he said. "Told you that you weren't walking in there alone."

"Yeah, but you didn't know you'd walk out promising to take a bullet for me."

"Think I needed McDade money to make that promise?" he asked. "You're a good kid. And just as screwed up as the rest of us."

She smiled and propped an elbow on the door. "You think Connel's okay?"

"I know he's at the club," Strat said. "Means either he's fine or he's…"

Dead? Dying? It didn't bear thinking about. He wouldn't, would he? Get himself that injured for her? For pride? It was becoming clear being with a man like Connel wasn't just unpredictable or extreme, it was dangerous too.

And she didn't mean for her.

Him. People would always come for him. Did she want to be the one sitting at home waiting for a call? Thank God their relationship was temporary. He'd said it was on until he was done with her. Should she be speeding that end along? If she got attached, how easy would it be to walk away?

FIFTEEN

WHEN STRAT STOPPED outside Stag, she leaped out of the car without saying a word. Yes, it was rude, but he knew she was worried. He'd get it. He didn't call to her… or at least she didn't hear him.

Security moved, letting her run inside, but when she got to the stairs, the guys there didn't budge, bringing her to a screeching halt.

"Move," she said, glancing back and forth at them. "Please."

"Not up here, sweetheart."

"Sweetheart?" she practically spat the word at him. "Get out of my way."

But when she tried to muscle through, they closed ranks.

"You're not getting in."

She stepped back. Neither of them were looking at her. No Daly to back her up. No Strat.

"Fine," she said, "forget it."

Except rather than go out, she went into the club. What the hell was going on? Ignoring the people and the music, she made a beeline under the office and went toward the spiral stairs.

Before she even got there, the guy on security moved aside and unhooked the rope barrier that hadn't been there when she went up with Connel. At least, she hadn't noticed it then.

Thank God someone was with the program. She ran up the stairs, crossed the balcony, and went into the living room. If he was laid up, he'd be in bed, right? But it was dark, no one was there.

He'd be in the office. He was always in the office at that time... if they weren't busy having sex.

She ran down the stairs or started to. Halfway down, she noticed Niall in the shadow at the bottom. As she inhaled to ask what was going on, he laid a silencing forefinger on his lips.

What the hell? Her confusion might have been funny, if a voice hadn't carried from beyond the curtain Niall blocked.

"...is not a free pass. You understand?" Shit. That was Lachlan. What the hell was he doing? "She's doing a job. That's it. Writing a story. Don't think no one's watching you, McDade."

Silence dragged on. She itched to go through there and get between them. Except her brother put her in the apartment and said goodnight on her promise she was going straight to bed. It wasn't a lie; she hadn't specified whose bed. Semantics. Maybe she was spending too much time in Stag.

"Anything else?" Connel asked, more bored than intimidated by what she could tell.

"You touch her, I'll come for you."

"Okay," Connel said like he couldn't care less.

"I'm not joking around."

"And I'm not laughing," Connel said, on the edge of his patience. Funny how well she was getting to know his intonations. She should, they spent enough time in the dark. "You think in my line of work I don't have people threatening me every day? Yours isn't the first leveled at me tonight, I won't lose sleep over it."

"She's my sister."

"She's a grown woman," Connel said. "Believe me on that." Her mouth dropped open. Did he have to add that? "Now I have a meeting, so if you don't mind, detective, my guys will see you out."

Which was the nice way of saying they'd kick him out. Why had he come? If it wasn't so embarrassing, she'd be furious.

Her fear for Connel helped by routing her emotion elsewhere.

The office door closed. Niall waited just a second before hooking the curtain aside to check the coast was clear.

She wasn't waiting anymore and squeezed around him before getting the nod. Connel stood behind his desk.

"Baby…" she said, rushing over to lay her hands on him. They went everywhere. To his neck. His face. His collarbone. There wasn't a mark on him. Not a single visible scratch. "What happened? Are you okay?"

"I have a meeting."

"I heard," she said. "I'm sorry about Lachlan. I didn't know he planned to come over here. I'll talk to him."

"As I said, I'm not worried."

Something seemed off. She couldn't figure it out. Maybe it was her brother, or her absence, or his fight with Evander… Or it could be the last three days had spoiled her and she'd forgotten professional Connel could be so aloof.

"I am," she said, sliding her hands up to link them at the back of his neck. "You could've been hurt.

What if Evander was armed? What if they outnumbered you? He's nothing. Don't give him the satisfaction."

"I don't know what you're talking about," he said, unhooking her hands while nodding at Niall.

The lieutenant came over to put an arm around her.

"What?" she asked as Niall led her toward the curtain. "What's going on?"

The office door opened and a parade of beautiful women came in, accompanied by a bunch of Connel's guys.

That was his meeting? A harem?

"You stay upstairs tonight," Niall said. "We'll put a guy on the stairs."

So she couldn't go down or the women couldn't get up? "Wasn't he expecting me back?" she asked. "He told me he—"

"Plans change," he said, pushing her toward the bedroom. "He's not kicking you out."

He walked away.

"And I'm supposed to be grateful for that?" she called after him but got no response.

Feminine laughter carried up to her. Bed. Did she want to sleep there?

They weren't a thing, hadn't spoken about fidelity and commitment. Still, being in his bed when there was a chance of him bringing another woman to it... Wouldn't be the first time. This time there were other guys involved too.

Yeah, probably best to pass.

Except... did she want to travel back to hers? Strat was probably on his way home and the Manzanis could be out for revenge. Clearly, from what he'd said to her in the hospital, Evander knew about her dalliance with Connel.

Tired and trying to be smart, it seemed rude to

overstay her welcome.

Purse in hand, she exited via the balcony to descend the spiral stairs with no intention of marching through the office like the offended girlfriend.

The security guy turned before she got to the bottom. He didn't unhook the rope, just shook his head.

"You're to stay upstairs."

"I'm going home," she said, pointing past him. "Not to party or cause a scene, home."

He shook his head again. "Don't want this ugly, do you?"

Stunned, the question physically hit her. "I don't want this ugly? Are you kidding me?"

"Just go upstairs and play nice," he almost pleaded. "The boss doesn't want you out here."

"Doesn't he?"

And with his gaggle of gorgeous women and his party boys, he would probably just love her to make a spectacle of herself.

No.

Turning around, she went back up the stairs. She wouldn't fuss. Wouldn't shout. Not until he told her what the hell was going on.

Though, if he tried to bring anyone to their bed later, she'd scream until the roof caved in.

He didn't want her out there? But he didn't want her for himself either. And people said women were complicated.

SIXTEEN

THE PARTY WENT on most of the night. Until she fell asleep anyway. Singing, laughing, chattering, there could've been fifty people down there. That didn't save anyone from the mood turning salacious. Some sounds definitely came from the playroom…

It had been there before her. Obviously Connel used it. Still, hearing others enjoy it somehow cheapened what they'd shared in there.

Maybe that was exactly his point. His way of demonstrating their association would be fleeting. That what they had was cheap. What they had wasn't special. Of course it wasn't. It was a bargain anchored in extortion and deceit.

Maybe they needed to have a conversation… or not.

Connel would have to take a ticket and get in line. Her to-do list was growing every minute.

She woke up alone in an empty club. Not for the first time.

No car waited on the curb either. Maybe some of

last night's women needed a ride home.

The Chronicler was her goal. After missing the previous day's meeting and dodging Steeple's calls all weekend, she needed to catch him up.

Good thing he had time because she'd barely paused for breath since entering her boss's office an hour ago.

"She vanished," she said, throwing up her hands before landing them on the back of the chair she'd only sat on for about thirty seconds on arriving. "Dorsey McDade was the apple of her father's eye. They doted on her. All of them did. And then, bam, gone, never to be seen again."

"Didn't think the McDades were the type to let that sort of thing fly," Steeple said. "What did the cops say?"

"I don't know. Lachlan's getting me into Records this afternoon."

"You talked to him about it?"

"I didn't get into details," she said. "He got the call about Evander Manzani being in the hospital before we could get into it."

"That's one we should follow up on fast. Vex will talk to you. Is he still in the hospital?"

"I don't know. I saw him last night," she said. "He's not talking."

Not about who was responsible anyway. Thank God.

"That was quick off the mark, even for you," Steeple said. "Who gave you the tip he was laid up?"

"I was out with Lachlan when he got the call."

"Right. Sure."

Looping the conversation back to the point, she wanted to avoid talk of Evander and get back to the mystery Strat fed her.

"So you know Errol McDade is the grandfather.

He had a bunch of kids, but three of his sons took prominent positions: Burl, Alastar, and Clancy. The last being Dorsey's father. Dorsey is the forgotten McDade child. Twenty years ago, one minute she's there, the next minute she's gone. I'm hoping the police investigation will give me more insight. The media barely covered it. It was headline news when there was no news, and then it just stopped. No one reported on it after those first days."

"Why?"

"I don't know. The police files should shed more light. Was it an abduction? An accident? Is she dead? Alive?"

"Was a body found?"

"Not that was ever reported. But here's the thing, Clancy McDade, her father… he disappeared less than a year later."

"He didn't disappear," Steeple said. "He's in California or Arizona or some place like that now… I think he was in New York with Burl for a while."

"The point is, he left the city. He was close to Silvio Manzani. But he walked away from Alastar to go to Burl… or wherever he went."

"You think something went down between Alastar and Clancy?"

"I don't know. Like I said, I want to get into the police files. Most of the news reports were just about the family. Even back then reporters were worried about publishing the wrong thing and ending up in the family's sights."

"The Manzanis had a firm foothold in the Midwest then. Alastar and Burl were busy fighting the other Irish families."

"And each other."

"Right," Steeple said. "Now I get why you're shadowing McDade. Does he talk about his dad or his grandfather?"

Her head tilted. "How do you know I'm shadowing McDade?"

"That guy hanging around here last week," he said, pushing back in his chair. "And Lach called this morning."

"Geez," she said on a groan. "Good thing I'm seeing him today. Makes it easier for me to kick his ass."

"You'll do that *after* he gets you into Records, right?"

"Oh, yeah, definitely."

"You seeing Vex again today?"

Not if she could avoid it. "I doubt it."

Except her boss seemed intrigued. "He could be out of the hospital, happier to talk than he was last night."

"If he's out, I'm not chasing him."

Though he might chase her if he thought the games had begun. Typical. Anxiety could become paranoia, and this was the day she didn't have a guard.

SEVENTEEN

LACHLAN DIDN'T APOLOGIZE for calling Steeple. And he told her straight out he'd gone to Connel the previous night. So she got to read him the riot act for that without revealing her eavesdropping. Thank God for his honesty, otherwise she may not have been able to work that in.

Her sibling issues weren't anything to lose sleep over. As her father put it, they were always standing in front of each other. She wasn't surprised her brother wanted to look out for her.

Yeah, she was pissed he went behind her back, twice, but she might have done the same thing if their roles were reversed.

The police records she'd spent the day submerged in were both enlightening and mystifying.

Still scribbling her notes as she ascended the stairs, she needed to get everything in some semblance of order and—

"Sersha."

She stopped and raised her head. The echo of her

father's voice was difficult to mistake.

"Dad?" she asked, continuing toward the stairwell landing where he waited. "What are you—" she paused. "Did Lachlan call you?"

"No," he said. "I called him and he mentioned you were here. Would you like to get dinner?"

"Have dinner?" she asked, coming to a stop in front of him. "That would be two meals in one week. Is one of us dying?"

"Can't a father take his daughter out sometimes?"

"Yes," she said, suspicious. "But I know you, Dad. There's a reason behind the invitation." He'd sought her out; this was no coincidence. "Be direct, Dad. You're good at direct."

On an exhale, he lost his smile and took her elbow to direct her into the corner. "Lachlan said you're working with the McDades."

"Yes," she said, hugging her notes to her chest. "So?"

"It's dangerous."

"I know," she said. "Lachlan's got you covered there."

"I am concerned for your safety, but…"

"But…? What?"

"Do you have access that law enforcement doesn't?"

Her brow dropped again. "I don't understand."

"McDade. Ire. He runs the family."

"I know."

"He runs this city."

She smiled. "Grandpapa might object to that claim."

"You're not naïve," he said, impatient. "I didn't raise you that way. Lachlan said you are shadowing McDade. What does shadowing mean? Do you sit in on meetings?"

Squirming, this was a line her family had never asked her to cross before.

"My job is not to spy," she said. "I'm not a crime or undercover reporter." Or a cop. "My job isn't to scurry back with details. If I do that, I don't get the access I need."

"This is not negotiable," he said, growing stern. "You cannot withhold incriminating information… if you do, you're an accessory."

Wow, the shock was visceral. "Are you threatening me?" she asked, tempted to push him away. "What the hell is going on?"

Her father did arrogant with the best of them. His pompous belief in his own righteousness meant more to him than his parental duty. But that truth didn't usually manifest in such physical and intimidating form. Attempted intimidating anyway.

"We know about his manipulation."

Terror spiked. "Whose manipulation?"

And had he seen the tape? Connel wouldn't have… would he?

"McDade's," he said. "He's manipulating city officials at the highest levels for his own gain." Shit. He knew that? "This is nothing new. Crime and politics have a history in this city. In the country. There will always be corrupt elements in any…" He shook his head. "It doesn't matter. Just give me their names."

Surprise jolted her. "What? Whose names?"

"The names of the people you've seen him associate with." He gestured at the pad and laptop she held against her. "You can write them down if—"

"I'm not doing that," she said. "I won't do that." His frown became a glare. "I won't, Dad. No. My professional integrity won't—"

"What about his professional integrity?" he

snapped. "Is that the line he feeds you? That he has pride in what he does?"

"I don't know why you're so mad. I thought you knew better than to put me in this position. You never have before."

"You may have crucial testimony for—"

"I won't testify," she said. "And you can't ask me to, the ethical implications—"

"And what are the ethics behind people being ruined? Against the integrity of respect for your city."

"It's his city too," she said. "No one wants to hurt the city."

"No, just the people in it," he said and stepped back. "I thought you were raised to do the right thing."

"I do a lot of talking about the right thing," she said. "It's not the right thing to abuse someone's trust. The purpose of my work isn't to point fingers. It's not about sneaking around and tying bows for the cops."

"The cops protect you. They protect your city. Keep you from harm."

It was difficult to contain her smile. The whole point of frequenting Stag in the first place was its safety.

"Do you think it will be safer for me if I drop a dime on Ire?"

"You will always be protected in this city," he said. "Your brother, me, and your grandfather—"

"That doesn't give me the right to screw people over. What I do requires access. If my subjects can't trust me—"

"What happens when your city doesn't trust you?"

He spun around to stalk a few paces and slammed a hand on the opposite wall. The harsh thud ricocheted off the concrete up the chimney of the stairwell.

"What is going on, Dad? If there's something

wrong…"

"There's something wrong when my own daughter chooses scum over her family."

"This is not my father asking," she said, hoping to calm some of the strain in his voice. "You're the superintendent and anything I tell you—"

"I am your father," he said, coming back around to bear down on her. "No one needs to know about this conversation. You can give me the information in confidence. No one needs to know."

"That won't stand up in court."

"No, but we'll know who to focus on. Who our enemy is."

"Ire has ears everywhere," she said. "You can't think anything I say to you, anything you say to others, will ever be confidential."

"Is that a hint?" he asked, peering closer. "Are you saying those close to me are involved?"

This was peculiar. His edginess was almost… "You're paranoid, Dad. I can't tell you who to trust or who to doubt. But I won't divulge anything shared with me in confidence."

The growl of anger in his countenance snapped, and he turned to march away, tossing the corridor door out of his way to leave.

Well, she'd disappointed him. Nothing new there.

EIGHTEEN

SHE KNOCKED ON STRAT'S front door and waited for him to answer. The moment he did, she went inside.

"Where have you been?" she asked, dumping her things on his kitchen counter and raising the Chinese food bag in the air before putting it down too. "I brought dinner."

"You my mother or my wife?" he asked, yawning. "'Cause if it's the second, we should have a conversation about screwing around."

"Ha-ha," she said, moving around the kitchen to get plates and flatware. "So I spent most of the day elbow deep in old police files."

"This Dorsey?" he asked, opening the fridge behind her.

"Yes," she said. "Reports from the first night of her disappearance are thorough. The cops are called, as you'd expect. They document the scene, no obvious disruption, take statements…"

"From?" he asked, putting an open beer down beside where she dished out food. "Her father and uncle?"

"Everyone."

Strat grabbed one box and a fork, ignoring the fact she'd just tipped food onto a plate. Oh well, at least she'd only dirtied one.

"And?"

She put the clean plate away. "Not much. No one saw anything, heard anything. No major clues. No extraneous fingerprints or footprints found. No real physical evidence at all… Of course, half the city was in that house before the cops were called."

"I'm sorta surprised they called the cops at all. They usually keep these things in the family… in a family like that."

"Right," she said, taking her plate over to the chair by the window and climbing on, folding her legs under herself. "Except this is a kid in pre-k."

"And the McDades wanted her back."

"And not reporting the disappearance looks suspicious later on."

"So when the school call in officials for this little girl who just vanished…"

"Maybe those officials would take a closer look at the family and their not-so-legitimate practices."

"Right," he said, "so they had to call the cops."

"Yes, exactly."

"And then what?"

"Then nothing. There's talk of searches in the surrounding neighborhood. They canvassed neighbors. No one saw anything. No one heard anything."

"People are trained to say that," he said. "They know better than to talk to the cops about the McDades."

"Right."

"It has to be connected," he said, forking up some noodles. "It has to be. No way a McDade goes missing and it's just a coincidence. It has to be connected to the business. No one would take the risk of upsetting the McDades just 'cause she was pretty. Even kiddie fiddlers value their lives."

"You'd think…" she said, sliding to the edge of her seat, food perched precariously on her knee. "Except you want to hear the juicy part?" Still chewing, he raised his brows in confirmation. She put her plate on an end table to lean over her folded legs. "They recorded the interviews."

"Probably so no one could be disappeared later on if the cops reported something the family didn't like."

"Maybe," she said, less interested in the why than the contents themselves. "They talk to Clancy, Dorsey's dad. Usual questions. Relationship with his daughter. Undue stress. Any enemies…" Strat smiled. "I know, right? So they ask him if there's anyone else they should talk to. Anyone who'd know more about Dorsey's life or might be a person of interest…"

She paused.

"And…?"

"This is where it gets interesting. Clancy mentions teachers, nannies, he's sort of vague, she had this friend and that… Then from absolutely nowhere, want to know what he says?"

"Goddamnit, yes," he said, stabbing the fork into his food.

"You don't want to talk to Silvio Manzani," she said, dropping back in the chair like she'd dropped the microphone.

He frowned. "Wait… What the hell has Manzani got to do with it?"

She threw up her arms in a shrug. "I have no idea! It was totally random."

"Did they talk to Manzani?" he asked. "Can't imagine they'd be dumb enough not to take that as a lead on something."

"I don't know. After that, everything just fades out. They put the investigation on the back burner. They take almost everyone off the case, reroute personnel, and the media stops following the story."

"That's weird."

"I know."

"You want to talk to someone non-official."

"Not a cop or a reporter," she said, "someone who'd have known what was going on at the time."

"On the street," Strat said. "Yeah. Someone knows something. I always figured they did. Maybe I should've paid attention to the gossip… There's always talk, even if guys don't know what actually went down."

"Rumors, whispers, speculation," she said. "That's what I thought too. We need a common denominator. Someone who'd know both families. Do work for the McDades and Manzanis. They'd be most reliable, right? To hear it from both sides?"

"I work for both of them. I mean, I have, used to. Not anymore."

"Yeah, but you've just admitted you don't pay attention. I need someone who did. Any suggestions?"

"Most guys I knew in the old days are dead or in jail…" Epiphany hit his expression. "Jail…"

"What?"

"You know what happened around that time?"

"What?" she asked, understanding his earlier impatient infuriation. "Tell me."

"Hell Manzani went down for murder."

"Helios?" she asked. "Evander's big brother? He's been in for… twenty years or something." Strat's eyes met hers. She gasped and grabbed the arms of the chair to bounce her ass to the edge again. "Twenty years! Dorsey's been missing for twenty years!"

A light bulb moment lit her friend's eyes. "I can't

tell you if the two are related, but there's only one person anyone goes to in this city if they've lost something."

"Someone who? You think maybe Clancy went to him about Dorsey?"

"Nah," he said, "this guy's a kid, thirty-something max. He wouldn't have been around back then. But if you want to track down Clancy, he'd do it. He'd be the only one capable. The only sane one capable anyway."

"Sane?"

"Anyone ever mentions the Huntsmen, turn and run, if you value your life, or anyone else's," Strat said. "They're insane and you need sane." Yeah, because there was enough insanity in her life already. "Guy called Quest is your best bet."

Subtle. Was that his actual name or a nickname? Knowing the city, it was probably the latter.

"How does he work?" she asked.

"I don't know how he does what he does, just that he's known for his perfect record."

"He always succeeds?"

"If you believe word on the street."

Which meant it was a hundred percent true or a hundred percent bullshit, no in between.

"Couldn't hurt to talk to him," she said, standing up. "Where can I find him?"

"Nowhere at this time," he said, eyeing her while eating.

"It's not that late."

"Your security team sure? You might not want to rock up to his place with them. Showing up with heavies puts people on guard."

"You're my security team," she said. "You didn't care I was unprotected all day."

All things considered, the day had been uneventful. Any day that didn't include a visit from

Evander was a good one in her book.

His brow descended as he put the food box aside. "I got a text I wasn't needed, figured Ire stepped up your security after his showdown with Vex. You know, got you the best."

She shook her head. "I woke up alone and there was no one outside." No one inside blocking her exit either, which Connel was capable of if he wanted her to stay put. "Last night, Connel denied all knowledge of what happened to Evander."

"And you believe him?"

"No, of course not, but it's protection. He's protecting me." So she wasn't forced into an awkward position with her father. Something she may have said was impossible before their staircase meeting. "I guess whatever happened, he's confident Evander got the message."

"Ire might be confident, but you know better," he said. "One skirmish won't get it through Vex's thick skull. You can't think otherwise after seven years." He was right. "Take tonight off, Scamp. I'll track down the tracker for you tomorrow."

"I have to write tomorrow. Update my timeline." Though she'd have to find it first. "I need to order my thoughts and list my unanswered questions. You think Conn will let me interview him?"

"Yeah, 'cause that wouldn't be weird," he said and shrugged. "I don't know. You know him better than I do… and have ways of persuading him."

"Right."

Which would cross the ethical boundary she was currently straddling, swaying this way and that. Sexual favors would make it wrong. Connel liked wrong. He'd be more inclined to agree if it was naughty.

Just as a frisson of awakening tempted her hormones, memories of the previous night cooled them fast. She didn't want to fight and didn't want to ask what happened. Yet she also didn't want to fall into bed with him like he hadn't just confused the hell out of her. They were great. Had been great. All weekend. Until he'd spun a one-eighty and taken up with other women right in front of her. Without inviting her. Not that she wanted to participate, but it was supposed to be the thought that counted, right?

"Want me to give you a ride over there?" Strat asked.

"No, I'm skipping Stag tonight." If she didn't have security on the street, Connel had his reasons for believing the trouble was over. "I'll grab a cab home."

"Why don't you stay here?"

"Here?"

"You have faith in your boyfriend, great. I don't. Vex's in the hospital now—"

"He's still in the hospital?"

"Yeah, he got into some riot with an orderly or something, tore his stitches, opened the wound… I don't know what, but he'll be in the next couple of days. My point was, his people aren't cooped up in a hospital bed. If they want to strike at you for causing this feud…"

"I didn't cause anything."

"Your apartment is the first place they'll look. I don't know why you're avoiding the boyfriend tonight, and I don't wanna know. I also don't want you hurt. We'll get a movie, finish the beer, and I'll take the couch."

Strat's place was safe and warm and didn't involve traipsing across the city.

"Okay," she said. "I'll stay."

"Good," he said on a nod. "Now go get more beer out the fridge 'cause mine's empty."

They shared a smile. Strat cared. More than her own father. Her friend wanted her safe, happy, healthy.

He'd become her rock. She couldn't even be as honest with Lachlan as she could Strat.

She valued him, their friendship, and would have to find a way to show him her appreciation for his support. Another thing to add to the to-do list.

NINETEEN

NEXT MORNING, the bedroom light went on. "Shit, Dad, I don't know why you—" Whose voice was that? Was it morning? Squinting into the intrusive light, she tried to get her bearings. "What the hell is this?"

Someone was standing just inside the bedroom door. Someone. Shit.

"Imogen," she said, holding the covers to her chest as she sat up. "Uh… hi."

"Hi?" Imogen said, propping a hand on her hip. "What the hell are you doing in my dad's bed?"

At that, the bathroom door opened and Strat joined them. Wearing nothing but a towel.

"Shit," she murmured.

Imogen made a sound of disgust. "Oh my God!"

"What you doing here, Immie?" Strat asked. "You okay? What happened?"

Typical that he hadn't even given thought to what his daughter might assume about the scene.

"She's younger than me, Dad!" Imogen said, her face scrunching in disgust. "Oh my God!"

Their visitor spun around to stalk out.

Strat just looked at her.

"Go after her!" she hollered.

"What?" he said, finally getting a clue this wasn't good. "What the fuck did you say to her?"

"Oh my God, Strat. I didn't say anything. She thinks we had sex!"

"What?" he asked, blinking in shock. "Why the hell does she—"

"Take a look around, Strat."

He did and caught up fast. "Shit." Seemed to be a lot of that sentiment going around. "Imogen!"

As he marched out of the room, she got up without a thought of showering. She just wanted to get into her clothes as fast as possible. Drama was everywhere. And this one wasn't on her. Not exactly.

How fast could she get out of there?

Her notes were spread on the kitchen counter. They'd have to go with her. The previous night, Strat talked her through the details he remembered. Not that he remembered much. His philosophy leaned more to staying in his lane than asking questions of the trigger-happy criminals who ran the city.

Tossing her hair from her face, she rushed out of the room and ran straight into Strat's back. He hadn't got far. Probably because his daughter was on the opposite side of the room, gesturing wildly.

"This is disgusting," Imogen said, throwing her arms up. "It's wrong. Totally wrong…" She snorted. "That's probably exactly why you want to do it. Is that what it was? The forbidden? You know she's the cop's sister."

"The cop?" she said, peeking around Strat.

"My idiotic father and brother refuse to say his name," Imogen said, then recoiled in disgust again. "Lachlan will go postal."

"No, he won't," Strat said.

Imogen was still addressing her. "I'm not telling him. You're telling him. Don't think I'll lie for you though. If you don't tell him, I'll tell him."

"You don't want to do that," Strat said, his voice oddly deep. "Immie—"

"Don't Immie me like that," she said, gesturing between them. "This is sick."

"Because there's an age difference?" she asked, just curious. Strat twisted to land a glare on her and she shrugged. "I want to know."

"Because you're younger than me," Imogen said. "He's old enough to be your father."

"He's a better man than my father," she said, much to the surprise of everyone in the room, including herself.

"Your father's Police Superintendent."

"I know who my father is," she said, squeezing around Strat to go to the counter and gather up her notes.

"You know he'll arrest you for something, Dad," Imogen said. "The police superintendent. When he finds out about this, they'll find some way to lock you up… Maybe that's not such a bad thing. Hell, even Lach will find some loophole to put you away."

"Who says it's anything more than sex?" she asked, scooping her things into her satchel.

"Don't," Strat said.

She glanced at him for a second before looking at the dumbstruck Imogen. "If it's just sex, my father and brother don't have to know. You think they know every guy I ever slept with? Does Strat know every detail of your sex life?"

"Just sex," Imogen said, still sort of on pause. "It's just sex?"

"I'm saying it could be."

"No, it couldn't," Strat said. "Nothing's going on, sweetheart."

"Don't baby me," Imogen said, returning to her disgust. "Don't remind me that your girlfriend was born after your own daughter."

"She's not my girlfriend," Strat said. "She's in trouble and stayed over because her place isn't safe."

"Oh, that's convenient," Imogen said, glaring at both of them. "Very convenient. So you just tripped and your dick fell into her?"

"We did not have sex," Strat said, measuring his words.

"Don't let her judge you," she said, folding her arms. "Don't let her judge us."

"Right," Strat said, turning her way. "'Cept your boyfriend won't see it that way, will he?"

The slight widening of his eyes reminded her they had to be careful of more than just Imogen jumping to conclusions. If, somehow, this got back to Connel, he might not wait to hear explanations.

"Right," she said, her arms dropping to her sides. "We're not having sex. Never had sex. He's just... helping me out."

"Great," Imogen said. "I totally believe you."

She totally didn't, but Sersha picked up her satchel, tossing the strap over her head. "You two have a great day.

"Just gonna disappear on me?" Strat asked.

She shrugged. "I have to go home and... you know."

"Call me later."

She nodded and offered Imogen a smile before slipping away. She'd go home to shower and change, then get to the library... and maybe the archives again. The jigsaw wasn't complete, but at least she had more pieces.

***

THE DAY HAD a horrible habit of sneaking away from her. She'd spent a big chunk of it on the phone trying to track down Clancy McDade.

Given Strat had his own problems, she wanted to take a shot at getting to the guy before involving the tracker. The fewer people who knew about her investigation before she got a chance to talk to Connel, the better.

She intended to loop him in after darkness descended and she got club ready. He hadn't called. She hadn't heard from him at all since his party on Monday night. Would she have to deal with that at the club? Maybe. But she couldn't put it off forever.

Getting a cab to Stag, she figured it would go one of two ways. Either Connel wanted her to react to his sex party or he didn't. If she didn't bring it up, he likely wouldn't either. Maybe letting it slide was the better option. Sex for silence was their deal. Despite Daly's view on the matter, theirs wasn't a monogamous relationship.

She paid the driver and got out, straightening her skirt before approaching the club. Connel would be busy or he wouldn't. She might not get to talk to him at all.

The head security guy held up a hand. "No."

"No?" she asked, glancing at the line of wannabe clubbers behind the rope. "You want me to line up with the others?"

Stopping just short of following with the cliché, *"do you know who I am?"* she was losing patience with the brutes Connel employed.

"Can if you want," he said, looking past her. "Still won't get in."

"I won't get in?"

"No," he said and opened his overcoat to retrieve something from his inside pocket. "He's finished."

What the hell was going on? "He's finished. What does that…?" The bouncer held out a flash drive. "He's finished." Understanding settled over her as she took the USB stick. For a second, she was just cold. Finished. Their deal was done. That meant… over. They were over. And he didn't even have the decency to tell her himself. So much for loyalty. Standing there on the street wouldn't accomplish anything. Swallowing, she moistened her lips. "Okay." Forcing a smile, she didn't want the guys to see her disappointment. "Thanks."

Did she really say thanks? Turning to walk away from the humiliation, her defeat didn't make sense. He was done? Because she hadn't called him? He hadn't called her. Maybe he'd been done since Monday. The sex party must've been a good one.

A car horn blared, startling her. She stumbled back, holding up a hand to block the bright lights coming right at her. Damnit, she was in the middle of the street. Waving in apology, she picked up her pace and kept on walking. She needed distance from Stag. From whatever had just happened.

Why was she so shaken? Stag had been her safety. Being barred from there was like being barred from her own escape. Now she was open, completely open, exposed, vulnerable, to anything Evander's heart, or body, desired, if he got his way. What was she going to do? Move in with Strat? With Lachlan?

Her eyes closed for a second. Her brother. Shit. She'd have to tell him everything. The whole truth. Evander's interest came and went through the years. Whenever she could shield her brother from it, she did. Now it was a thing again, maybe worse than ever before.

According to Strat's contacts, Evander was still

in the hospital. After what he'd said to her… Evander thought there was a contest or something going on. She didn't blame Connel for wanting to be free of it. She wanted to be free of it too. Shame it wasn't so easy for her to walk away.

The whole thing was ridiculous. Evander was a cocky—

A hand closed over her mouth as an arm locked round her ribcage, hauling her off her feet. She kicked and tried to scream, but there was nothing as whoever he was lugged her into shadow. She couldn't breathe with his huge hand blocking her airway. What the hell was…? Who was…? Shit. Think. Breathe.

Slammed back against a wall, the air rushed from her lungs. Pain blasted the back of her head. Stars dazed her eyes.

A gruff voice, right in her face, fogged her with foul breath. "Talk," he snarled. "Fucking talk."

"What the…?"

Had he asked something? What was happening? The dark air smelled like urine and dumpster. An alley. They were in an alley.

"McDade," he hissed. "Who's on his payroll?"

"Who's on his—"

Yanked forward and thrown to the ground, something hard hit her side. Searing fire shot up the inside of her arm. Screaming at the pain, she somehow ended up on her back.

"You tell me who the fuck he's greasing."

"I don't know what you're talking about," she said, cradling her aching arm. "I don't know what you want to—"

"Think he'll protect you?"

Her hips moved, her dress. Fuck. Cold, slimy hands groped her thighs, yanking fabric, jerking it up to her panties.

"Where's the fucker now?"

"No," she said, fighting to close her legs when a knee landed between them.

"Fucking talk or he'll have you."

Closing her eyes, she sucked in a breath. Concentrate. Don't be afraid. Be smart. One guy crouched over her, dirty blond hair, blue eyes…

"Do you know who my father is?" she panted, huffing in one breath after another.

The grit of dirt dampened her skin, her dress, her hair. When someone grabbed her thigh, she kicked out with the other leg. Up and out, just like Lachlan taught her, leading with the heel. From the howl of pain, she guessed she hit the mark.

"Fucking bitch!"

"Get out of here. Now," she said, finding her disgust in time with her rage. "You don't want to get in any deeper."

The dirty blond guy laughed and glanced at his colleague. "You hear that? She's threatening us!"

Skull and crossbones tattoo behind his ear.

"I'll fucking show her."

Her thighs were grabbed again. She fought, using all her strength to close her legs as a shorter, stockier guy tried to get between them.

"Fuck you," she said, kicking though she'd lost both her shoes. "No!"

"You want him to stop, you tell us," the blond guy said. "Who's McDade got on the council? His allies. Who's on the Harvest deal? Tell us!"

"Fuck you," she said, spitting at him.

Flipping over, she tried to crawl away. Someone grabbed her ankle and dragged her back. Emptying her lungs, she screamed. Someone had to hear her. Please. Anyone.

"Dumb bitch!"

"No!" she yelled, scrambling to grab for something, anything.

Trash and puddles. No weapons. No salvation. When they let go of her ankles, she struggled to her knees, desperate to get to her feet.

A fist tightened in her hair, jerking her hard, swinging her around in an arc that ended in the harsh brick of a building. Nausea. The pain was more than her body could handle. She couldn't see anything but black. Still, she lashed out, nails first, seeking skin. Gather the evidence. Lach would need evidence.

Another something hit her gut and she doubled. Lachlan. Tears would come if they could. One hit became another, and she was on the ground again. Retching. Screaming. Trying to fight. Her brother… He'd never forgive himself. He'd never let this go. She'd be his demise.

TWENTY

SHE WANTED TO PUKE. Her body convulsed. Every part of her ached.

"Lach."

Her voice was dry, her throat scratched.

"Hey! Hey, she's awake."

Someone grabbed her hand; another rush of pain. Her head throbbed, but she rolled it to try blinking the figure next to her into focus.

"Lachlan?"

"I'm here," he said, his kiss warming the back of her hand.

She couldn't really see him. Or she could, but the edges blurred, slipping in and out of each other in the glare of light.

"I'm not dead."

"You're not dead," he said, tightening his grip.

Recoiling wasn't possible, but her other hand was heavy. She couldn't even lift it. "Where am I?"

"Hospital," he said. "You scared us."

"Us?"

"Was it McDade?" Lachlan asked. "He did this to you?"

Did what? Focusing was a struggle.

"No," she said, trying to frown. "No. No… What's going on? I don't… Where are we?"

"Don't rush her."

Her attention moved to that voice. "Grandpapa?"

"We're all here, Ser, honey." Someone touched her leg over whatever covered it. "We're here for you."

"Who is…? What?"

"She's disoriented," Lachlan said.

"Yes, she'll need time to recover." Was that her dad? "Don't rush her."

"We need a statement," Lachlan said. "I need to know who to take down."

"Don't talk like that." Yes, her father. "The investigation will need to be impartial. You shouldn't be anywhere near it. None of us should."

"He tried to kill her."

"We don't know that. We don't know what happened."

"Ser will tell us," Lachlan said. "Sersha, honey, what happened? You were only a few blocks from McDade's club."

From Stag. She remembered going there… but she hadn't got in.

"My head hurts," she said, closing her eyes.

"Your injuries are severe," her father said. "You have a concussion. Torn ligaments in your wrist. Bruised ribs—"

"Don't scare her," her grandfather said. "Give her time."

The alley. The attack.

"The docs need…" Her brother's voice was somber enough that she opened her eyes to try seeing him again, but she still couldn't distinguish much in his features. "They need consent to do a rape exam."

"Oh, God," she groaned, warm heat slipping from her eyes when she closed them.

"We don't know that she was raped."

"We'll get him," Lachlan said, taking her hand higher. "Whatever it takes, honey, you know I won't stop until he's off the streets."

Swallowing again, she parted her dry lips. "They," she croaked. "There were two of them."

"Two?" Lachlan asked, odd hope in his voice.

"Can I have water?"

He let her go and stood, then he was directing a straw between her lips. "The more you can tell us, the easier it will be to track them down. Take your time. Tell me what you remember." The pain in her head pulsed every time she sipped. "They've got you loaded up on pain meds. Tell me what you can and then you can rest."

"She might not want—"

"Yeah, but she might," Lachlan snapped.

Her brother snapping? At her father? Maybe she'd woken up in a parallel universe.

"Lach," she said, releasing the straw, her hand rising and flopping down under its own weight.

"I'm here."

"I want you to… stay here."

"I'm staying," he said, grabbing her hand again. "I'm staying, honey. I'm not going anywhere. Tell me what you remember."

She tried to shake her head. "Lach."

"What, honey? I'm here."

"Just us."

"Just… Everyone clear out."

"No, we're not—"

"Go!"

"We'll go," her grandfather said. "We'll be just

outside."

Movement and door sounds followed, but she couldn't concentrate and kept her eyes closed, attempting to relax and steady her breathing.

"I hurt everywhere."

"I'll ask them to up your meds," he said. "I don't know if they can, but I'll ask."

She managed a smile. "If you ask the nurses, they will. You're a stud around here."

"Guess you're feeling better."

Not on the pain scale and her memory was fuzzy, but she remembered her brother. And being there with…

She frowned, rolling her head on the pillow in his direction. "Is Evander still here?"

"He's on the fourth floor. I checked. As far as I know, he doesn't know about this or that you're here." That wouldn't last. "I won't let him hurt you. Was he involved?"

"I don't know," she said, trying to keep her head still. It hurt more when she moved. "I don't know what…"

"Just tell me whatever you can. Is there something you didn't want to say in front of Dad?" There was plenty she didn't want to say in front of their father. "Is it about the assault? What they did to you? Do you remember…?" His pause was ominous. "Were you raped?"

"I don't know," she said, details blurred. "I think I passed out."

"You hit your head hard. More than once. Do you consent to the exam? I know it will be uncomfortable, but the more evidence we can gather—"

"I scratched him," she said, still disconnected from her arms somehow. "At least one of them… I think."

"Good."

Her lips curled again. "The first guy was tall. Over six feet… I kept trying to focus. I knew you'd want a description… When they started… I thought maybe I wouldn't make it out and scratched him, so—"

"Hey," he said, his thumb moving on her cheek, swiping away the free-falling tears she hadn't noticed. "I will get him. I promise you. No matter what it takes."

Except she didn't want to break her brother's good heart. "I shouldn't have been walking there."

"Why were you?"

Pain between her eyes intensified. "I don't know, I can't remember. I remember I was… He came from nowhere. I didn't see anything. Not a… I didn't see anything; I was just picked up and… we were in the alley."

"It's okay. Take your time."

Sealing her lips, she inhaled through her nose, fighting to quell the nausea. "I need you to do something."

"Okay."

"You might not understand it, but… I need you to do it."

"Whatever you need. What is it?"

She took another fortifying breath. "I need you to tell Strat to come in."

"Strat?" he asked, confused. "Kurt Stratford? Imogen's dad?" She managed a slight nod, her eyes still closed. "Why would he…? What do you mean come in?"

"If he's heard, he won't be far away," she said. "And he'll have heard."

"How is he connected to this? Did he hurt you?"

"No," she said and forced her eyes open. "Please, Lach. Please ask him to come in and talk to me."

"Okay," he said, none the wiser as he rose to take his phone out. She assumed anyway, it was just a black blur. "I don't have his number. I'll need to call Immie."

"Great," she said, closing her eyes.

So if he didn't already have the story from Imogen's point of view, he'd get it then. Dumping one shock on another.

"Hey… No… No… Thanks… Listen, can you… Yeah, how did you know…? Okay… I'll tell her." A moment later, he picked up her hand again. "Im says you should get better soon." Wow, okay, so she didn't hate her guts. "And she already knew you'd want her dad. Want to tell me what's going on?"

"Another time," she said. "You should go tell the doctor people I consent to the exam before I pass out again."

"Are you dizzy?"

"My vision's blurred… I feel sick."

"I'll tell the doctor, but—"

A door burst open. "Scamp."

She smiled. "Strat."

"What the fuck?"

"I know." He grabbed her heavy hand, sending a shudder of searing pain up through her arm. "Ow, don't do that."

"Shit, I'm sorry."

"Strat," Lachlan said. "Want to tell me how you're involved in all this?"

"Go talk to the doctor," she said, using all of her energy to squeeze his hand. "I need to talk to Strat for a minute."

Her brother would be confused. Of course he would. But he kissed her hand again and retreated to depart.

"What the fuck happened?" Strat asked, striding around the bed to grab the hand Lachlan had held.

"Are we alone?"

"As far as I can see, yeah," he said, sinking down,

probably into a chair. Had Lachlan been sitting? "You were on your way to Stag? Why the fuck were you walking—"

"I was at Stag. I mean, I got a cab there and… He's done with me. We're through."

"Wait," he said in a puff of breath. "Tell me he didn't do this to you."

"No," she said, using his grip to pull herself up a little more. He adjusted her pillows, helping her sit straighter. Nausea washed over her again. She breathed until the worst of it passed. "You need to talk to Conn."

"Okay, want me to kick his ass?"

If her torso wasn't so sore, she might have attempted a laugh. "No. I don't. I need you alive."

"He break your heart?"

"No," she said. "We're over, that's fine. You have to tell him they're on the edge."

"Who?"

"I don't know," she said. "I don't know who it was, but they wanted information… I didn't tell them anything, but whoever they are, they're getting desperate. Tell him it was about the Harvest deal."

"The Harv…Shit, Scamp…" He let go of her hand when he surged to his feet. "They hit you because you're a McDade? He cuts you loose and then you get your ass handed to you for being his girl?"

"It wasn't like that. It doesn't matter," she said. "If it wasn't me, it would've been someone else. And that's the point. If they're desperate enough to lean on an alderman's granddaughter, they'll lean on others who aren't so well-protected. He needs to shore up his defenses."

"You're worried about him?" he asked. "This is way more than leaning on you, Scamp. You should be fucking mad."

"I think you and Lach have got that covered,"

she said without the energy to muster any kind of emotion. Maybe the pain meds numbed those too. "Please just tell him." Her next request wasn't so easy. "And I… there's something else."

His frown returned. "What?"

"Do you know where it happened?" Even she wouldn't be sure which was the right alley. "Where they…?"

"I can find out."

Licking her lips, her mouth was drying again. "I was carrying a flash drive."

"In your purse?"

"It wasn't in my purse." Had they stolen her things? The purse wasn't important. "I need you to find that drive… please. Find it and hide it."

"What was on it?"

The door opened behind him and a guy in a white coat came in with a woman in scrubs. "How are you feeling?"

"Sick," she said and tugged on Strat's hand. "Please."

"Okay," he said and kissed her knuckles. "I'll take care of it."

"Strat, thank—"

"Don't worry about it anymore," he said. "Consider it done."

He backed out of the way to let the doctor get close. Once he'd left the room, all the tension she'd been holding dropped. Her friend needed to think she was strong. That this would bounce off.

"Your brother said you consented to the rape exam." She nodded. "I can do it or the nurse can."

"Whatever," she said, closing her eyes. "Just do whatever you need to do."

"We need to ask if you've had intercourse in the last seventy-two hours."

The last seventy-two hours? She wasn't sure she could count to seven, let alone seventy-two. "Monday," she said. "I don't know what day it is."

"Thursday," the doctor said. "Did you use protection or is there a chance—"

"We used a condom," she said, refraining from adding *"a lot of them."*

"Okay."

"But it was…We got rough sometimes."

"Not this rough," a sympathetic female murmured.

She smiled at the woman standing by the end of the bed.

"Did he force you?" the doctor asked.

"No!" she said and winced. "No, I just wanted to… if there's bruising down there, it doesn't necessarily mean…" Her throat closed. Shit. Why was she…? At least this time she noticed the tears. "I'm sorry."

"Don't be sorry," the doctor said. "We'll just get set up."

To investigate her body. To poke and prod and… How could a life change so quickly? She'd been fearless and forthright. Always willing to push herself and there, in that moment, she couldn't even say the words.

It would get easier. It would.

TWENTY-ONE

AFTER BEING IN the hospital for two days, she was more than ready to leave.

Uncomfortable, she tried to move, which wasn't easy with her arm in a sling.

Lachlan came in with a file. "Hey, what are you doing?"

He came rushing over to prop her back against the pillows.

"Moving," she said, wriggling in the sheets. "I want to get out of this bed."

"They might discharge you in a day or two."

"You think I don't know you and grandpapa are pressuring them to keep me here?"

"You're important to us," he said, kissing her head. "Why shouldn't we use our pull to make sure you're looked after?"

"Yeah, but it's not a medical request. You're just being protective," she said, nodding at the file as he sat. "What is that?"

It didn't look thick. Was that the sum total of

their investigation?

"It can wait a minute."

"Just tell me," she said. "You want me to ID someone?"

He rolled his lips into his mouth. "Yeah," he said on a sort of inhale.

"Okay, so show me."

"You don't want to rush yourself."

"You've been telling me to take my time for two days." The nausea wasn't as bad, though she did still get bouts of dizziness. "Between you and Steeple telling me to take it easy, I'll never move or work again. Just show me."

"I don't want you to be shocked," he said, opening the file just enough to peek into it.

"Shocked? Why would I...? You mean you don't want me to get upset?"

"No, it's..." He hesitated then sighed. "The subject's deceased."

"Dece—he's dead?" she asked.

He nodded, folding back the cover of the file to hand it over.

Blond guy. Swollen. Bruised. Cut. Bleeding. Well, not anymore, but there was blood on his face.

"He has the tattoo," he said, reaching over to slide another picture out from beneath, putting it on top. "Is it him?" She nodded, numb, as he took the file from her hands to close it and put it aside. "He was killed last night. Showed up in the early hours."

"Showed up where?"

"Why would you ask that?"

His curiosity got her attention. "Why wouldn't you tell me?"

"At Silvio Manzani's. Strung up by his ankles in a tree, on proud display outside his front door." A beat passed. "It wasn't pretty, Sersh. Whoever killed him was seriously pissed. Seriously pissed."

"What do you mean?" Grabbing the file, she wanted to see what made her brother so solemn. "How did—" She stopped at the next photograph. "Oh my God."

Lachlan took the file before she could see the other pictures. "They emasculated him, disemboweled him, antemortem, Ser. I don't know what the perps wanted him to give up, but he wasn't a willing victim. Every one of his fingers was broken. Not that it mattered, 'cause they cut off his hands and scattered them on the driveway with his toes and teeth like ice-cream sprinkles." Her mouth wouldn't close. It was amazing, disgusting, yet not repulsive. "They tortured him. Cut out his tongue. There were over two hundred individual injuries on the body. Then they somehow got him into that tree and cut open his stomach, spilling his guts all over, while he was still alive." Though probably not conscious. "No one saw anything. No one heard anything. Silvio's people are locked down."

"So you think it's something to do with the Manzanis?"

Did it shock her brother that the grizzly scene didn't upset her? It did because it was vile, but so was the man. He deserved everything he got.

It took Lachlan a minute to clear his throat. "He's still a John Doe, but he worked for someone and had the Manzani mark."

"First Evander, now this guy," she said. "The Manzanis dealing with a coup?"

Intrigue twitched in his eye. "That's the second time you've referenced the Manzanis turning on their own. What do you know?"

"I know the Manzanis." Unfortunately. "They're power hungry. All of them. And ruthless."

"Same could be said of a lot of people in this city.

In the world.”

"True," she said, smoothing the sheet on her lap with one hand. "It's just my opinion."

"Your educated opinion," he said. "You know these families."

"Sometimes I do," she said.

"You may not be a criminal underworld expert, but you know the Manzanis."

"Some of them."

"What about the McDades? Anything from them?"

"Nothing," she said.

"You never told me why you were so close to his club."

"I don't want to talk about Connel."

"You know nobody calls him that."

"It's his name."

"You're the only one who calls Evander Manzani Evander too. For most he's Vex."

"He's Vex because he pisses people off everywhere he goes. That's why he always has someone at his back," she said. "He could just keep on being him while his guys or his brothers paid his debts and bailed him out."

"One of those brothers is in prison."

A serendipitous tangent to explore. "Do you know who worked that case?" she asked because it was relevant to her investigation. "Helios Manzani's conviction?"

"Not off the top of my head," he said. "Want me to look into it?"

"No, but you could get me into Records again."

"They don't like people just wandering in off the street."

She flashed him a smile. "Yeah, but I'm the superintendent's daughter."

"Has Dad been here much?"

"He calls the nurses' station. They let him know how I'm doing."

"Henry's been in."

She smiled again. "Grandpapa's here every day. I think he likes the photo op on the stairs. I keep seeing him in the news."

"Yeah, I'll tell him to back off."

"It's okay," she said. "I'm not front-page news."

People cared how an alderman spent his day. They weren't so worried about his granddaughter. Probably because she'd told Steeple to get word out she didn't want a big deal made of it.

The door opened. She expected her grandfather. Maybe Strat, though he'd already been in. Instead, it was a nurse with an enormous bouquet.

"Oh God," she groaned.

"Wow, secret admirer?" Lachlan said, standing up to take the arrangement the nurse could hardly see past.

"Not so secret," she said.

"Is there a card?"

Her brother may have been asking the nurse, but she answered. "Let me guess, Evander got out today."

"Evander Manzani? Yes," the nurse said. "Earlier. Did you get your dinner?"

"Someone came and took the plate a while ago," she said, omitting the fact she hadn't eaten much.

"Do you need anything, Detective McLeod?"

Her brother was straightening the flowers and took a second to process his name. "Oh, uh, no, I'm good. Thanks."

The young woman smiled and departed.

"Ooh, big, strong, handsome detective," she teased in her best Marilyn voice.

"Cut it out."

She laughed. Probably for the first time since the attack.

"Oh, oh, Lachlan. You're so pretty and so strong."

He dropped into the seat again. "You think I work out for the job?" he asked. "Nope, it's all about the pussy."

Her nose wrinkled. "Okay, you don't say that word. It doesn't sound right coming from your mouth."

Now it was his turn to laugh. "A lot of other women don't feel that way."

She had to smile. "Have you even been with someone since Immie?" she asked. "You're probably Mr. Fifth Date."

"Mr. Fifth Date?"

"Do you even go in for the goodnight kiss before the fifth date?"

"According to you, I haven't been on a fifth date for years." He squinted toward the ceiling. "I can't even tell you what Im and I did for our fifth date. No, I can actually. Dinner… there was definitely some action."

"On top of the clothes action?"

"More than a kiss anyway."

"You don't remember."

"I remember our first time," he said.

"Before or after the fifth date?" He smiled, which made her laugh. "See! I knew it! You're Mr. Respectful."

"And that's a bad thing? You don't think there are enough scumbags around?"

"Yes, there are definitely enough scumbags."

"I like to sleep at night."

"Rather than worry about the women in your life?"

He got serious. "I'm worried about you."

Suddenly, nothing was funny. "You don't have to worry about me."

"I know Dad's always giving you crap about finding a guy. But… I kind of agree with him right now."

"Please, you are not serious!"

"You don't need a guy to pay your bills or get you pregnant, but I would feel better if there was someone next to you at night. The cops were called because a stranger heard you screaming. That was lucky. Pure luck. If they'd got there two minutes later…"

"I'm alive."

"Yeah, but if the cops weren't called, and you were left there… How long until someone found you? Until someone noticed you were missing."

"I was never missing."

"But no one was at home to notice you weren't there, that you didn't come home."

"Being with someone just to be with someone doesn't interest me."

"I know and I want you to be happy with whoever you end up with," he said. "Still… I'd feel better if you stayed with me for a while."

"I don't want to cramp your style. Where would you take all your nurse groupies?"

"It's that or you stay with Dad."

"He's home less than you are," she said, "and wouldn't notice whether I was there. He didn't notice when we did live together." Her brother couldn't even argue. "I'll be fine at home. Strat will check in."

"I'm still getting over the fact you hang out with him. You know he hates me, right?"

"He doesn't hate you… Maybe he hates you a little… I always say nice things about you."

"That makes a huge difference, I'm sure."

His phone rang. On instinct, he moved to answer it, but checked himself and hesitated.

"It's okay," she said. "Go. Go."

Her brother would be protective for a while.

That came with the territory. She'd keep up the facade. Be strong. Because that was what he needed to see. Maybe it wouldn't be so bad. Actually, it was what she needed. She'd never felt more vulnerable, more exposed. She just had to keep telling herself to get through it. Be strong.

***

WAKING WITH A START, darkness unsettled her. Lachlan was gone. She must've fallen asleep while he was on the phone.

The hospital was quiet. People moved beyond the room. Phones rang. But she was in a secure area… She felt secure anyway.

"We need more information."

She gasped, her head snapping toward that brogue.

"Niall," she whispered as he approached from the shadowy corner.

"Did he have an accent?"

"What? Who?"

"You said dark hair and stocky," he said, coming over. "Look at these guys."

Light from a cellphone signaled the device in his hand. She was still getting over the fact he was there.

"What do you want me to—"

He turned the screen to her and started swiping through images of guys on the street, one in a bar, one in an alley. Different guys, different places.

"Stop," she said, closing her eyes. "I don't know who it was."

"You don't absolve these guys, none of them will get mercy."

"What does that mean?" she asked.

It wasn't easy to discern his features with the

cellphone light in her face and the rest of the room in darkness.

"No one comes for a McDade without repercussions."

"I'm not a McDade," she said. "He finished with me."

"Look at the pictures," he said, swiping again. "Point to the guy who hurt you. It's one or all, Sersha."

And that was a warning to heed. Setting her focus, she eased his hand away and swiped, looking at each face in turn until she stopped. She didn't even need to scrutinize it; she recognized him immediately.

"That's him."

Niall glanced at the screen while switching it off to put it back in his pocket. He just walked away, no further instruction or explanation.

"Wait," she said when his fingers landed on the door handle. "What happens now? Are you going to kill him?"

"No," he said like he was shooting the breeze. "Ire is."

He left. Even as the door sank back into the frame, she just stared. Ire? Was going to…? He couldn't mean it. Why would he do that? For her? For whatever he was protecting? She'd probably never know.

TWENTY-TWO

IN HER BATHROOM, she popped open a medication bottle. "Pain meds," she said, smiling at the pill in her hand. "As long as I can take pain meds, I'm fine."

Those were the words she'd said to her brother before kicking him out of her apartment a couple of hours ago.

Strat showed up not long after and she'd told him the same thing.

In her apartment, behind a locked front door, why wouldn't she be safe? Especially given she had it on good authority her attackers were being taken care of. Not that she told Lachlan or Strat.

She'd have to be alone sometime. Would have to learn how to do basic things, even with her wrist immobilized in a splint.

In the hospital, she'd wrapped her forearm in a plastic bag and the nurses helped her shower and wash her hair. How she'd get by without their assistance remained to be seen.

For the first time, she was getting a look at

herself. One eye was black and swollen. Bruises covered her forehead and cheekbone, disappearing into her hair. The jagged line of blood by her temple was a testament to her torture. When did that happen? When he slammed her to the wall the first time? When he threw her to the ground? Maybe it was as he dragged her back along the concrete.

Bruises and scrapes adorned her body. They'd heal, eventually. What went on inside her head wouldn't be so easy to get over. She brushed her teeth with one hand and dragged a soft brush through her hair.

She'd wanted out of the hospital because she was sick of lying in bed. Now she was desperate for it.

Her silk robe was short and easy to pull on with its wide sleeves. Tomorrow she'd need to find shorts and some tanks to wear for sleeping. She wasn't used to wearing anything in her own bed. Maybe it was being alone, but she just didn't like the idea of being naked at all anymore.

She'd never thought about her wardrobe in terms of what could or couldn't accommodate a sling. Stupid little things like cuffs and seams had never featured in her thoughts. Now they were important details.

Turning off the light, she opened the bathroom door. One step into the bedroom, the sight of a figure by the other door stopped her dead.

His identity registered fast. "Conn…" she said on an exhale. "Don't do that. You scared the crap out of me."

"You shouldn't be alone."

"I shouldn't be alone?" she asked. "Why not?"

"Get your shit together, we're getting out of here."

"What? To go back to Stag?" she asked, shaking her head. "Doesn't work for me."

"Who the fuck do you think you're talking to?"

he said like he couldn't believe her insubordination. "Get your damn shit—"

"No! This is my home. I won't let them chase me out of here."

"You don't know what you're dealing with," he said, striding over. "I'm taking care of this. Taking care of you."

"No," she said again, her resolve slipping as her breathing grew shallow. Closing her eyes, she backed up a step and came up against the bathroom doorframe. "You should go."

"Why?" he asked, his fingers combing into her hair, scooping down and around until he cradled her chin. "I'm sorry."

The gentle murmur was so startling, her eyes opened to his. "For what?"

"I swear they'll pay for what they did to you."

"You already killed one guy," she said, though didn't know what happened to the second guy after her identification condemned him.

"It's not enough," he said, tipping her chin higher. "I will hunt down every person they ever cared about. Every minute of every fucking day, they'll pay for hurting you, for touching you."

"The people they cared about didn't do this to me," she said. "I know who did this to me. You know who did this to me. You know why."

"Because you're a McDade," he said, keeping hold of her chin while his other hand stroked and finger combed her hair. "You didn't surrender."

"If I had, they'd just have killed me."

"Macushla," he breathed, descending to rest his mouth on hers.

The gentle need fractured her defenses. Her hand rose to his neck, clinging to him as her lips parted and his tongue slipped past them. The safety, the security of Stag, was in that kiss. She'd needed this steadfast, stalwart of shelter to be herself again, to be free, to be protected.

Except he'd taken it away. He'd stolen it from her and could do that again, any minute he chose.

"No," she said, planting her hand on his chest to separate them.

"Let's get out of here."

He took her hand and started to move, but she stayed put. "No," she said when he looked back. "I appreciate you being worried about me, but I'm staying here."

"You do what you're fucking told."

"No," she said, her hand slipping out of his. "Not anymore." His jaw tightened. The heat of fury rose in his eyes. "I'm not scared of you, Conn. Even after seeing all the terrible things you did to the asshole who hurt me, I'm not scared of you." Just in case he was thinking about showing her that anger. "You don't want me to be afraid of you."

"You think I can't force you?"

"No, you can," she said with a slight nod. "But you won't. You want my consent. You want to be in charge, but you want me to want that." His lips thinned again. "You want me to submit. Voluntarily."

How many times had he told her she wasn't a prisoner? With the video, even when he had the upper hand, he didn't force her. He got satisfaction in her choice to give him the power.

"I told you I would look after you."

"Then cut me loose."

"Is that why you're—fuck, forget it. You're coming with me!"

"No," she said again, pushing away from the doorframe. At that moment, it was important to defy him. It was important to show him she had power too.

"I won't just forget that. I can't just forget it. You said our agreement ran until you were finished. You're finished. You gave me the video. It's over."

His gaze darkened. "You think I don't have copies?"

"Is that how you want to play this?" she asked. "Make like we're repeating history? No."

"No? No! You don't say no to me," he snarled. "No one says no to me."

"I do," she said, getting up so close her sling met his torso. "I say no when you're wrong. You're wrong, Conn."

He grabbed the hair at the back of her head in a sudden tight fist. Sharp pain shot through her skull; the sting hissed out between her teeth.

Immediately, he relaxed his grip. "Macushla," he whispered.

"Quit saying that," she said. "I don't even know what it means. Accept that things are different now. If you think this is necessary, that I'll share or print anything I saw in my time at Stag if you don't keep me sweet, you can relax. I have no intention of divulging your secrets."

Or theirs.

"If you were going to spill, you'd have done it to the guy beating you."

Her chin descended as her eyes closed. "I'm tired, Connel. I want to go to sleep."

"You sleep in my bed. Where you're safe."

"I'm safe here," she said. "Lachlan will call and check in. He's pulled strings to route patrols this way too. I'm safe."

"Not as safe as you'll be with me."

"And the next time you want to have a party? The next time you get bored and replace me with some bimbo?"

"You don't know what you're talking about."

"Maybe I don't," she said. "We talked about trust, but we didn't have it. We never trusted each other, not really. And why should we?"

"You proved yourself."

"Oh, is that what I did? Great! Thanks for the test."

"It was nothing to do with us. I did not set those guys on you."

"I know that," she said. "I also know it happened on McDade territory, right on your doorstep. That why you dumped the body on Silvio? You're pissed they came into your territory and touched your toy. Except I wasn't your toy, not anymore, because you finished with me."

"I found your goddamn notes," he snapped. "Whatever the fuck you were writing about Dorsey."

"Oh," she said, no less affronted. "And you didn't think it was weird they were right there in your office, probably lying on your desk? I wasn't hiding anything and I'm not ashamed of what I was doing. If you'd talked to me about it—I actually planned to talk to you about it. You dumped my ass before I got a chance."

"We had the weekend."

"Yeah, and talking was so high on the agenda," she said on a semi-scoff. "You have no idea what…" Clarity was an odd creature that visited at random moments. "You dumped me because you thought I was writing about your family. That what? I was using sex to manipulate you?" Probably something he'd faced before. "Shit, Conn, how often did we talk? You didn't let me get close. You kept me a football field away from you. I was always less interested in the story than I was…" Not something she wanted to say out loud to him. "If I wanted McDade secrets, it would've been easier to manipulate Niall or Daly with sex. Hell, I could've slept with Hock or Snuff, any of the guys you had driving me, protecting me. You don't think they'd have been an easier mark? You think I'm so low… that I'm such a cheap slut, I'd use my body to get a story?" She laughed, just a short, humorless exhale. "I do something you can use against me, you do something I can use against you. That was the basis of our relationship. I don't go to that guy for protection when I'm scared. I don't turn to him for comfort when I'm low. You don't give a shit about me, not really. You sent your guy to the hospital, you didn't even come yourself."

"For you," he growled.

"For me?"

"You've been ashamed of this from the start. You don't want anyone to know this exists."

"That's okay," she said. "Because it doesn't. Not anymore."

"I don't give up," he said. "You're a McDade."

"You can say it as often as you like. But if that was true, I wouldn't have been anywhere near that alley, would I? I wouldn't have been unsafe in your territory."

"You'll never be unsafe again."

She sighed. "Go home, Conn. Go back to your world and leave me in mine."

"It was real," he hissed.

"Our attraction? Yes," she said because it was impossible to deny. She wasn't ashamed of it either. "We had fun. It was fun. But this is real life, Conn. This is my life. I need people around who are real. People I can rely on. People I can trust. I need people who care about me. Who'll be around for a long time. You're not that guy."

"I've killed for you," he snarled under his breath.

"For me?" she asked. "Or for your pride?"

Seconds passed, his eyes flashed to hers and then he was gone, slamming the bedroom door at his back.

Breathing out, the adrenaline got a chance to sink in, and nausea hit. Dropping back against the doorframe, she closed her eyes, waiting for the dizziness to pass. At least this time she could check something off the to-do list. Connel was out of her life; she'd never have to deal with him again.

TWENTY-THREE

PUTTING HER ARM in a plastic bag was the easy part. She'd never realized just how much she needed both hands in the shower until she was without one of them. Even putting the cap over her hair, so she didn't have to wash it, was difficult.

It would be her life for a while, she'd get used to it.

Clothes were more difficult. Pants would be no problem, but nothing work suitable fitted over her splint. So she went with a dress, maybe a little formal, but she would rather be more business than pleasure.

She tried with the concealer, but it was impossible to hide the swelling still in her face. In the mirror, she didn't look like her. Was that her injuries or something else?

Whatever it was, she had to get back to her life and left her bedroom ready to return to work.

She didn't expect there to be people in her living room or for one of them to be her former protector.

"Daly?" she said.

He turned to smile at her. "Miss me?"

"What the hell?" she asked, glancing at Strat next to him before hurrying over to hug the other bodyguard.

At least, she intended to hug him until she raised her good arm too high and aggravated her injuries.

"Don't worry," Daly said, offering a gentle hug. "I know I'm out of shape." He didn't look bad at all, considering. "I've got guys downstairs for the tough stuff. Boss just thought you'd prefer a familiar face."

"Strat is familiar," she said, looking at him. "What's going on? Why the hell are you here?"

"I'm here because I knew you'd never do as told and rest," Strat said. "Didn't expect McDade to answer the door when I knocked."

"McDade to… Connel?" Her focus swung back to Daly. "Why was Connel in my apartment again?"

"Again?" he asked. "Boss spent the night."

"Boss spent the night," she murmured. Shock hit her hard. "He stayed over?"

Daly snickered. "Guess it wasn't a night to remember."

He'd walked out of the bedroom. She hadn't actually seen him walk out the front door. Had Connel McDade spent the night on her couch? No. Why would he…? Because he wanted his people to think he was a stud? No, he didn't care what people thought. If he wanted to be a stud, his efforts in the playroom when there was an audience would prove his prowess.

Thank God Lachlan hadn't come over before Strat. Her brother had left a voicemail when she was in the shower, but she'd already texted him to say she was alive and well.

"I'm going to work," she said to neither of them specifically. "I want to check my email, see if any of my efforts bore fruit."

"You can't check your work email here?" Strat

asked.

She smiled. "I can. I just don't want to."

On the night of the attack, her intention was to spend the night at Stag. She had cash in her purse, but not her wallet or cards. Which was great, given her purse was long gone. Lachlan got her a new key for her apartment. Everything was as it should be. Wasn't it?

"Need a ride?" Strat asked.

"We have a car," Daly said.

"So does Strat," she said, heading for the door. "I'll get in the car with him."

She could get a cab, but Strat was her friend. She wasn't trying to send him a message.

As soon as they were in the car, he asked, "What happened?"

"Oh, God, you know," she said, putting on her seatbelt as he got them going. "I'm so sick of that question."

"McDade came over?"

"Yes," she said. "In the middle of the damn night."

Though, in fairness, she didn't know exactly what time it had been.

"Seemed like you didn't know he was there this morning."

"I thought he went home," she said. "I told him to go home."

"You told him to leave?"

"Yes."

"And he didn't force the issue?"

Shifting in her seat, she angled toward him. "Why are people always so surprised he's not violent with me? No, he didn't force the issue. He could've, but no. I told him to go, and I thought he did."

"But he stayed."

"Apparently."

"And you're okay with that?"

"Not really," she said, flipping down the visor to check her eye in the mirror. "But what am I going to do about it? It's done."

"Daly and his people are following us."

Flipping around, she looked over the shoulder of the chair. Yep, the Bentley was tailgating.

"Shit."

"There's a whole van full of guys behind it," he said. "Ire's serious about protecting you."

"Protecting me from what, exactly? Evander followed me around for years. Never once did anyone gunning for the Manzanis come for me."

"You blame him?" Strat asked. "The attack was Ire's fault?"

"No," she said. "It wasn't his fault! It was..." That was an interesting point. "Who was it? If they were Manzanis..."

"Vex was pissed about you and Ire."

"If Evander wanted to hurt me, he'd do it himself," she said. "And no one mentioned my physical relationship with Conn. They wanted information. Business information." Her attention stopped on his profile. "What's the Harvest deal?"

"Beats me," he said, glancing at her. "I thought you knew."

"No. I'd never heard of it until they mentioned it."

"Except they thought you knew enough to screw it up."

"I think they wanted it screwed up," she said. "I did have information."

"Did you tell them?"

"No," she said. "What good would that have done? Then I'd just have two families after me."

"That's why you didn't tell them?" he asked, his

gaze lingering an extra second. "That was your first thought?"

"Honestly? It happened so fast, I don't know why I didn't tell them. They were more interested in beating the crap out of me than waiting for an answer. The second guy was…" Saliva rushed her tongue; she swallowed. "If they had the Manzani mark, they were loyal to the Manzanis."

"Could ask Vex," he said. "Find out what he knows."

"Go to him voluntarily?" She shuddered. "Is that a game I want to play?"

"McDade spends the night, then the next day you seek out Vex… He might be looking for you."

"Evander?"

"If the attack wasn't on his order, he can't be happy someone acted without his consent. He thinks of you as his girl."

"One of them," she said. "When it suits him."

Her inquisitive mind wanted to know more, but was it worth it? If Evander didn't give her answers, Connel was her only other potential source. Unless she asked Daly. He had been laid up for a while, as far as she knew. He might not know about the Harvest deal and could get in trouble for mentioning it.

"If Manzanis hurt you and you go to them… It might not end well."

And she was definitely not in fighting form. "Maybe I should focus on one mystery at a time."

"Probably a good idea. Want to stop somewhere for breakfast?"

"No, please," she said, her stomach roiling. "I can't even think about food."

"You've lost weight," he said. "Wasn't much of you to begin with. You should be eating."

"I have a brother to lecture me about that. He's

got you covered."

They shared a smile. Strat wanted to look out for her, she got that, appreciated it. Better him than Lachlan. Though, really, she didn't want anyone putting their life on hold for her.

When they got to The Chronicler building, Strat said he'd be around if she needed a ride later. She didn't even talk to Daly, though the Bentley stopped behind them. Maybe he'd be there all day… or maybe he'd get bored and leave. Wishful thinking.

Another huge bouquet awaited her at The Chronicler reception.

Lucy leaped to her feet. "Oh, Sersha! Hi! Oh, God…" She came around to hug her, too tight, she braced against the pain. "You look so good."

"Okay, that's a lie," she said with a smile. "But thank you." She nodded at the flowers. "Addressed to me?"

Lucy nodded and went back to her post. "They're so pretty."

"Keep them," Sersha said. "Keep all of them. Or give them away to good causes."

"I don't get it," Lucy said, her head dropping to the side. "He really loves you."

"He doesn't know me. Any messages?"

"A bunch!" Lucy said, grabbing a stack of notes from her desk to hand them over. "How can someone who doesn't know you love you so much?"

"Exactly my point," she said, looking through the stack.

One man showed his love with flowers, the other used mangled corpses. Did either of them really know her? That wasn't fair, Connel never claimed to love her. His murder spree was about the family name, not winning her heart.

She turned to head for Steeple's office but didn't

get a step before her head spun. Grabbing for the reception desk, she squeezed her eyes closed, searching for stability.

"Sersha!" Lucy exclaimed.

Someone held her arm and helped her to the floor to sit. Sitting was better.

"Thank you," she said. "I just… moved too fast, I think."

"You shouldn't be here."

A male voice. A familiar one.

She opened her eyes to confirm the ID. "Daly."

"Didn't think I'd go far, did you? Want to get out of here?"

"No!" she asserted, trying to get back to her feet. God only knew where the notes had gone. "I'm going to my boss's office."

"Okay," he said.

Suddenly, someone scooped her up off the floor. "What the hell are you doing?"

Daly again. Goddamnit. Was he even allowed to carry people? How injured had he been?

"Boss says to do whatever you need."

"Well, you tell him I needed to have screaming, wild sex right in the middle of the bullpen and I forced you to oblige."

He laughed. "Yeah, I wanna keep my life. But I can call him if you—"

"Don't even think about it."

Without knocking, he opened Steeple's door. Her boss spun in his chair, phone to his ear, and frowned the moment he noticed them.

"I'll call you back," he said and hung up to leap to his feet. "Ser, what's wrong?"

"Nothing is wrong," she said as Daly settled her down in the seat opposite Steeple at the desk.

Daly offered a two-fingered salute and went out,

closing the door, though he stayed right there to block it from the outside.

"This guy again?" Steeple said, wary as he descended to sit.

"Don't," she said on an exhale. "It's not me, it's Conn—I'll talk to him, tell him to call his people off."

Though without her phone, calling to converse might be difficult.

"Will he?" Steeple asked. "Do you want him to? No offense, but I don't feel worse knowing they're watching your ass… Unless it was McDade's people who jumped you."

"It wasn't."

"She says with authority without telling anyone who was responsible."

"Lachlan call?"

"A couple of times," he said. "I don't blame him for being worried."

"I've been lying in the hospital for four days and chose not to crash your meeting this morning so my return wouldn't be a big deal. But I'm here. I want to get back to work."

"What does McDade think about that?"

"Who the hell cares what he thinks?" she asked. Rage didn't help her injuries, but it was automatic. "Don't dare tell me he called—"

"If Ire McDade called this building, I'd give him the damn keys," he said, touching his collar. "You know he's killed people, right?"

Cautious, she didn't want to be paranoid. "Who told you that?"

"No one told me. It's known. People know that. Guy gets mad in a snap. You must've seen it."

"He doesn't…" She took a second. "He cares. About the family. About his people. He's protective of them."

"Hence the guy on the other side of the door."

"Daly is one of his people. Conn cares about him too."

"And you? Does Ire care about you?"

Angling her head, her boss's curiosity didn't escape her notice. "I was attacked in McDade territory."

"So it's a personal insult? He doesn't care who you are, just that someone stepped on his toes?"

So many people wanted her to talk about things she couldn't make any sense of herself.

"Can I hang out here today or not?"

"Sure," Steeple said, pushing back in his seat. "Just don't do too much. Having your brother on my ass is one thing, put against Ire McDade…"

"Okay," she said, standing up. "Thank you."

Given she'd about passed out at reception, doing too much would be impossible, even with all the will in the world. Still, for as long as she was able, she wanted her mind busy and not obsessing about other things, other… people.

TWENTY-FOUR

DESPITE ARRIVING LATE at The Chronicler office, she was wiped by the middle of the afternoon. A little thing like tiredness wouldn't get in her way. She took more meds and soldiered on. Daly was nearby, watching her. Watching. Watching. Any hint of weakness, or clue she needed help would be reported back to his boss. Connel was one person she didn't want showing up anywhere near her life.

Her eyes were closing, her head drifting, her concentration had been gone for over an hour. What time was it? Catching her head on another drop, she blinked at the wall clock. Six thirty. Yeah, that was it, she was done.

She should call Strat and—

"Ser?"

Daly stood behind her shoulder. Had he noticed—he held out a phone. Her phone. Connected to… someone.

Taking it from him, sidelining questions about where he found it, she put it to her ear. "Hello?"

Daly was already walking away.

"Sersha?"

"Conn, whatever—"

"You wanna see him?"

"See… who?"

"The scum who put his hands on you without permission."

Her chin rose; exhaustion vanished in a flash. "You have him?" she breathed out.

"Want me to finish it fast…? Please don't ask me to finish it fast."

She surged to her feet. "Where are you?"

"Daly will bring you."

"We're on our way."

She hung up and turned.

Daly strode over. "We going?"

"We're going," she said, shutting her computer down. "Fast."

"You got it."

They were downstairs and in the car within a minute. She didn't know where they were going or what was at the other end, other than Connel and her attacker.

Why was she going?

Yanking the liquor from its slot, she held it between her legs to pull out the stopper. Forgoing the glass, she drank from the bottle. Sure, her splinted arm didn't help, but she didn't care about decorum. Who was there to see her anyway?

How would she look into the eyes of the man who'd wanted to rape her? Blond guy was dead. Finished. This other guy… She could call Lachlan. That would be the responsible thing to do. Her brother could have the perpetrator arrested. He'd gather evidence, they'd go to court… She gulped more liquor. What would prison time mean for this guy? More connections, more skills. He'd come out to a Manzani hero's welcome.

She swallowed. What was she capable of? What did Connel want her to do? Anything? Nothing? Witness her attacker's death?

All she knew was she had to get there. She had to be there.

Stag. Before they even stopped, three guys in black came to the curb, waiting to open her door to usher her out. Daly stayed with her as they went inside, past the stairs, into the club and around to the back of the bar. Behind the wall of optics and colored bottles, a wide passage narrowed to a single door. They went through that, took a turn, another door and down. Down into the darkness. Into a large square hall with doors leading off it.

The guys closed around behind her, guiding her to the middle of the space. A door to the side opened and Connel joined them, giving his guys a discreet signal to leave, which they all did. Some went back the way she'd come, others went through the door Connel appeared from.

"You know what happens down here," he said, coming close enough to cup her face. She nodded. "You can walk out of here any minute, any second. You don't have to be here for this."

"I want to be," she whispered, stepping in to rest against him, laying her palm on his chest. "I don't know why, but I do."

"Because he violated you," he said, his brow creasing. "Because he touched what didn't belong to him. Because he…"

His head snapped to the side.

"He didn't rape me," she murmured, sliding her hand up to his jaw to bring his attention back to her. "He didn't. They checked."

"He thought about it," he snarled, bowing a fraction lower. "That gets him a death sentence in my house.”

"This doesn't change things between us," she said, stroking his stubble. "I meant every word I said last night."

"It's not about us," he said, though his hand skimmed around to splay on her back, forcing her against him. "If you need this, you get this. I can kill him quick if that's what you want. I'll bring you his head. I'll do it, Macushla."

"I still don't know what that means."

And he didn't enlighten her. "You remember what I said about rules here?"

"Rules don't exist here."

Those were his words.

"Anything," he said, his eyes narrowing in certainty as they came closer. "Whatever you want to do, whatever you want done, it can happen here. You won't be denied anything. No one will tell you to stop. No one will say no to you. As long as you're in that room with me, you rule the McDades. You are our leader."

"Don't," she said, her eyes drifting shut. Emotions were high and intoxicating adrenaline flooded through her. He was intoxicating. Somehow, their chemistry took over. She could feel him in every intimate nook like he was arousing her again. "I promised myself I'd be strong." And that was turning out to be a pipedream. "Conn…"

"You are strong," he said, his lips grazing her temple. "I am with you."

Is that why she was strong? Did his power give her strength? Yes, it did. Had in the past. His fingers found their way between hers to guide her into a long, dark corridor. About halfway down, they paused at a door.

"Conn," she whispered, tugging his hand before he could open it. "Is he… tied to something?"

For a second, he assessed her, then his brow came down again. "He won't touch you. He won't get anywhere near you. But, yeah, he's strapped to a chair in the middle of the room… He'll stay there until you say otherwise. You're safe." He turned to her again, jerking her chin up. "You're always safe with me. Tell me. Where are you always safe?"

"With you," she said. "I won't let you down."

Though she had no inkling of what would happen in the room beyond. He kissed her head and opened the door. She held her breath as they went inside.

She expected a dank cell. Yes, it was dark, but the room was clean. The floor was a paler gray than the walls. Men stood in each corner. Off to the side, a table bolted to the floor. The canvas over it concealed whatever was underneath.

But it was the man in the middle of the room, his ankles shackled to a metal seat, his hands behind his back, no doubt restrained somehow, that drew her keen focus. His head stooped, his whole body sagged forward.

Connel said something in his other tongue and the guy in the furthest corner came to stand behind the prisoner. No mistake, that was exactly what he was.

"Show respect!" Connel demanded.

The guy standing guard kicked the chair hard.

The prisoner snorted and raised his head. Bruised and bloodied, it was clear she wasn't his first visitor. Her instinct when his eyes met hers was to step away. And there was Connel at her back, holding her up, his hand sliding onto her shoulder.

"This fucking bitch?" the prisoner spat.

The chair got kicked again. Somehow, he jolted, though the chair didn't actually move.

"You didn't know…?" Connel said, his voice dark and heavy. "You put your hands on my woman, Pietro."

A flash of surprise crossed the prisoner's face. "You—your woman?"

Another order came in Connel's mother tongue and the guard grabbed the guy's hair to yank his head back, exposing his throat.

Her inhale wavered when Connel wrapped an arm around her to hold her against him as he kissed her head. His strength was her foundation. The cornerstone of her stability. That power remained even when he slipped away to whip the canvas from one end of the table to the other. She didn't look, just heard it and then he came into view between her and this Pietro, a blade in his hand. Curved and shining, the precision tip at the end of the eight inches of gleaming metal was terrifying.

"No, no," the guy said, his head jerked back, harder, the strain of his voice came out in a whine before words. "I didn't—I didn't know! I didn't!"

"Send them out of here," she murmured. Connel stopped just a couple of feet from Pietro. "I don't want anyone else here."

Connel gave an order, and the four moved for the door. The one behind the chair threw the prisoner forward so hard only his restraints caught him.

Once the door was closed behind them, Pietro started again. "We didn't know. How could we know?" The guy coughed, his body sagging forward again. "You killed Carl."

"Aye," Connel said without hesitation. "He begged too."

The confession was unexpected. But this guy wasn't leaving alive; it didn't matter what they said to him. He'd never be free to utter the truth to anyone.

"You want power," she said, her voice quiet. "You like exerting power… But you're powerless. You're powerless now. How does it feel?"

"If you're gonna kill me, just do it."

"You giving my lady orders?" Connel asked and lunged down, driving the blade into their prisoner's thigh, wringing a howl of pain from strained lungs.

His sobs of pain didn't reach her or rouse compassion. Connel's fist tensed around the handle.

"Leave it," she said before he could pull it out. As asked, he let go of the blade and backed off. "I'll fucking show her…" The memory sent a shudder through her, but she suppressed it to walk closer. "You said, 'where's the fucker now…' and 'I'll fucking show her,' didn't you?" So many details were foggy, but the crisp menace of his excitement was crystal clear. Crouching down just in front of him, her heart pounded, but she wasn't afraid. "Look at him…" He didn't move. "Look at Ire and tell him you challenged his authority." Her voice was so calm, right until his lack of a response infuriated her. Grabbing the handle, she twisted it hard. "Look at him!"

She screamed over Pietro's wail of agony. But she got his attention because he raised his head enough to find her gaze.

"Don't fucking look at her!" Connel shouted, marching over to grab Pietro's hair and force his head higher. "You look at me!" One swift punch followed another. "Obey her fucking orders!"

She got up in a twist to walk away and took a second before turning back to the men. "You thought you could follow him? That scum like you had the right to touch what was his? How in the hell could you possibly believe you'd ever be able to take from him?" Moving again, she went around behind them and kept on going in a stroll. "Challenge him now… Sneer at him the way you sneered at me… You want to taunt someone, taunt him."

"I didn't know," Pietro wept. "I didn't. Ire, I swear to you!"

Connel wrenched the knife from his victim's thigh but offered no reprieve and immediately plunged it into his shoulder. Another howl of pain. Connel's eyes rose over Pietro to find hers.

Was he worried about her being scared? Horrified? She should be. Some part of her would be. But this was perverse therapy. Taking her power back from one of the men who stole hers, it renewed her somehow.

"I don't want to touch him," she said.

"You don't have to," Connel said, straightening up. "Whatever you want, Macushla."

In that moment, there was only one thing she wanted.

Avoiding the blood pooling on the floor beneath the chair, she went around to be met by Connel.

"Conn…" she breathed.

On a low growling laugh, he hooked an arm around her, yanking her against him. "That fucking voice."

"He wanted to touch me," she said, pushing her palm up his chest. "Think we should untie him and let him try again?"

The pride that lit his eye was almost amused. "Please gimme that order, baby."

She smiled. "Maybe I should order you to fuck me instead. Let him watch how a real man pleasures his woman," she said and accepted his mouth when he swooped down to kiss her.

She wasn't sore. Wasn't in any pain. He held her close, pressing himself to her, his arousal imprinting itself on her stomach.

His mouth trailed to her ear. "Whatever you want. Anything."

Bowing back, leaning on his supporting arm, she was drugged on them. "Does he deserve to know us like that?"

"He doesn't deserve to breathe."

"And he won't," she said. "He wanted power over your woman in your territory."

"He has to die."

Feathering her fingers down his cheek, she touched his lips with a fingertip. "To protect what's yours."

"You don't have to… I'll work for you," Pietro pleaded, but they were lost in each other. "I'll do whatever you want, McDade. I'll tell you stuff. I know stuff. Silvio… he wants to buy them out. To get in under you. He'll do it. He won't lose, won't admit he's losing his grip. Even his kid doesn't respect him."

On the night they'd met, she'd sailed in the green of Connel's intrepid gaze. He'd caught the man who hurt her, restrained him, and given her carte blanche. It was a valuable trust that opened her eyes to the man he was within.

There was more. She got it. His life was filled with conspiracy and betrayal. She hadn't betrayed him, even when her life was at stake. At the time, in the alley, she hadn't considered what signal that would send to him. Now she got it. Beyond humility, there was a bare gratitude shining down on her that revealed how he valued her. Did he mean it? Maybe not. It was intense. Always intense. In that room, they were tying their fates together. He could ruin her; she could ruin him. Leverage. That neither of them would ever use. The innate connection held them to each other, bonded them. What he'd done for her… he'd never know how cathartic it was to hurt the man who hurt her.

Maybe she'd feel differently tomorrow, but in that moment, every part of her was certain. Of what? She didn't know. Whatever it was, her purpose lay in him.

Pietro was still babbling, pleading, begging.

"Want me to finish it?" Connel asked, touching her cheek.

"Let him bleed out slow."

One side of his mouth lifted. He bowed to kiss her before winking and leaving her to return to the victim.

The victim.

The blade plunged into flesh; Pietro cried out in agony. She couldn't pity him. Her empathy well dried up. She'd begged, and he hadn't cared. Where was his empathy then? Where was his humanity? His single-mindedness on the night of the attack betrayed his not only willingness to rape, but an excitement about it. He must've done it before. Every woman he'd violated was in that room as Connel finished their attacker.

"You want to see?" Connel asked before coming around to her. She just shook her head. "Come with me."

He led her out of that room and into the next one along. A restroom. Metal sinks lined the wall.

"Wash your hands, scrub under your nails."

Easy for him to say. Her sling made that impossible. "I, uh…"

"Come here," he said, joining her at the sink.

From behind, with his arms around her, he wet his hands and washed hers between his, even using the nail brush to scrub under her nails. Almost like her hand was his.

His concentration was so intent on cleaning her up, she didn't have to do a thing and got the chance to process. The night they met, she'd said he was dangerous. She'd never once considered he might use that danger, those skills, to help her.

When he was done, he kept her hand to pull her to the wall and grabbed a towel to dry both of them off.

"Take off your shoes," he said.

She did, only to be surprised by him directing her

to a new pair by the door. Two together, one for him, one for her.

He'd planned it, known it would happen. If she'd said no, what did he lose? Nothing. She'd left things in his closet upstairs. Maybe he got rid of them; the shoes suggested otherwise.

He linked their fingers again to exit and return to the square hall where people were waiting. People that included Niall and Daly.

"It's done," Connel said. "Take him to pieces."

The others went down the corridor, leaving her with the three men she knew.

"Get the car and the guys," Connel said to Daly, who nodded and went upstairs. "We need a bundle." This time Niall left, putting her under the scrutiny of the only man left. "I don't want you home alone tonight. Daly will stay in your apartment with you. He'll call Strat to—"

"I don't want to go home." Honesty was risky. More so the longer he just looked at her. What did he see? What did he want to see? Could he be finished with her again? After what they'd just done together… "Do you want me to go home?"

His hand rose to her face. "Aye," he said, though it didn't feel like he was talking to her.

He did? That deflated her. When he walked, jolting her along, she went in a kind of blind mist up the stairs and through the club. Stag would open soon. Life would go on. It would just go on like nothing was different.

They went down the exit corridor. She expected him to leave her and go upstairs.

Instead, he continued outside to where Daly was holding open the car door for her.

Connel eased her into the backseat and closed the door to talk to Daly. Niall came out and joined his colleagues.

Home. Was she supposed to sit and wait for Daly to be done? Was he complaining about babysitting duty?

She couldn't even run her fingers through her hair on both sides. What had she done? She hadn't even thought to look for cameras or… but she hadn't caused the most damage. He had. And he'd done it in front of her. She was the only living witness. She'd told him they didn't have trust but didn't know a more irrefutable way to show it. Murder. What would someone want to conceal more than that? Yet he'd trusted her with it.

The back door opened. Connel surprised her by sliding in next to her, forcing her to the middle seat.

Daly closed the back door and disappeared from view.

"What's going on?" she asked. "I thought I was going home."

"You are."

Like last night? "I didn't know you spent the night at mine. As much as I appreciate—Lachlan will probably come over. I don't want to hide you in my bedroom closet or something. That's ridiculous."

"We're not going to your apartment. Unless you need to pick anything up."

"I have pain meds in my bathroom."

"Drugs are not a problem, babe," he said, wry in the declaration.

Well, yeah, drugs, legal or illegal, would be easy for him to get his hands on.

She had a bottle in her purse, which should still be somewhere in the car. "I don't understand. If we aren't going back to mine and we're not staying at the club… where are we going?"

"Mine," he said, reaching over her to snag her purse, which was apparently right there. Her head was so not in the game, any game. "Text your brother. Tell him you're fine and going to bed early."

"Yours?" she said, retrieving her phone to do as he said. "I thought the club was yours."

"It is. Sometimes I don't leave for days. Call it my second home."

"Second?" she said when he looked at her. "You have a first home?"

"I'm going to take care of you."

Like he'd said last night too.

"I'm not a prisoner."

"No," he said. "Don't you feel free with me?"

In so many ways, his lack of rules was liberating. Yet there was security too. A comfort in his attentive embrace. In the power he held. How far would he go with her? For her? He'd killed for her, twice. Rather than repulse her, that fortitude seduced her. This man, the one sitting at her side, probing her with his certainty, knew no limits.

"I do. Take me to your place."

He exhaled. "Aye."

TWENTY-FIVE

BY THE TIME the car got to wherever they were going, her eyes were closed. It wasn't until he moved from beneath her head that she awoke.

"Can you walk?"

"What?" she asked, shaking her hair from her face. "Yes, sorry."

He got out first and opened a hand to help her out. The towering building they went into barely registered. In the gleaming white hall, the elevator was the only option. They got in, he input a code and then they were ascending. Where were his people? His guards? His guys?

At the top, they got out on the opposite side and had only one option again, a broad black door maybe ten feet ahead.

"Locks are easy to pick," he said. "Here, we use a fingerprint and a code." Which he did. That was interesting. Or it might be if her head wasn't fogged. As she went inside a few steps, her eyes sank shut again. "Come here."

He swept her feet from under her. As she braced to fall, his body supported hers, carrying her across the sleek living room, upstairs to a bedroom. A huge room. Massive black blinds were closed over the full-height two story windows.

"You spent days in the hospital…" he said, tossing her onto the bed. "In bed, recovering…"

Her shoes disappeared, and then he was looming over her, easing the sling from her arm.

Blinking, her hand curved around the back of his neck.

"No, baby," he said, on what might have been a dark snicker.

Her zipper was down, her dress off, he was stripping her. That was okay. It felt good to be in the cocoon of his bed, firm, warm, soaked in his scent.

"Conn…"

"No," he said again, drawing her panties down her legs. "We're gonna take a shower. Stay there."

Where would she go?

Black sheets, pillowcases, comforter. Red McDade stag head embroidered in the corners. Not so different to his bed at Stag. Pushing her feet into the bed, she boosted herself up toward the pillows.

"No," his command stalled her.

Disoriented, a light came on to the far right and there he was in a doorway, naked in silhouette. She'd prefer to see more of him. She hadn't thought about sex or how she'd react to being seduced. Maybe because Connel hadn't been in her life since the thing. It had been too soon after him to think about anyone else. Then again, as he said, she'd only been in the hospital. When would she have had the chance?

"Get up." Another command. "Come on, on your feet. Front and center."

She didn't want to… Rolling over, she caught her

weight on her chest, trapping her injured arm. Pain. She was so sick of being in pain.

He came stalking over, bag and tape in hand. "You can't even stand up on your own and you're thinking about sex."

Stuffing her arm in a clear plastic bag, he tore a length of duct tape from the roll with his teeth and secured the opening against her skin.

"I don't need to stand up to have sex," she said as he scooped her up to carry her into the intrusive light. "And I wasn't thinking about sex."

"I know your voice, Macushla," he said, sliding open the glass shower door to take her inside.

The water was already on. Warm. Steam opened her pores. He sat her on a built-in tile seat in the corner.

If she was more awake, she might take advantage of her position, or think of a good comeback to his certainty.

Something cold hit her head and then his hands were in her hair. "I haven't had sex since…"

"You're running on adrenaline," he said, massaging her scalp. "You can't jump back into life like nothing happened. Your body needs time to heal."

"I don't have time to heal," she said, closing her eyes when soapy liquid slid down her face. She inhaled the water and reached out, her hand landing on his hip as she coughed. "Conn?"

"Tip your chin up," he said, but his hand was already under there doing it for her, then he was massaging her scalp again.

Water, soap, massage… He was shampooing her hair. Blinking her eyes open, her webbed lashes didn't hinder her view of him there over her, gathering her locks onto her head. The stern scowl darkening his brow contradicted the gentle care of his hands.

"Are you mad at me?"

His eyes jumped to hers. "No."

"You're frowning."

"I'm thinking."

"About?" As his scowl became a glare, he rinsed her hair. "This is all fucked up. It's so completely wrong." When the water cleared, he was crouching in front of her, razor in hand. "Oh, God, no, don't do that."

His grip on her ankle tightened. "My rules."

What was she going to do? Fight him off? In his bed, she'd prefer to be smooth. When her wits returned, she'd be embarrassed to be stubbly in his sheets… Though him taking care of her needs may be more embarrassing.

"You don't need to shave my legs, I can—"

"I'm gonna shave more than that."

"Oh, God," she whined, her head bumping back against the wall. "Conn."

"Enough," he said, the whisper of his lips touching the inside of her knee as he propped her instep on his shoulder. "Are you afraid?"

"I'm not afraid of you, Conn. I'm never afraid of you."

"Where are you always safe?"

"With you," she said, surrendering on a sigh.

His lips caressed her skin again. It didn't feel sexual; he took care of her, probably out of necessity. After she relaxed, it felt good to be completely in the care of someone else. While he was in control, she was calm, relaxed, completely content. There were no worries. Nothing to fear. No insurmountable problems. She was his, in his power, under his management. Connel McDade had the wheel. All she had to do was enjoy the ride.

TWENTY-SIX

"WHAT TIME IS IT?"

How long had she been lying there looking up at the ceiling far above? In the bed, alone, the luxurious comfort tempted her to stay. Except she was in someone else's home… and thirsty.

She got to the edge of the bed, his side probably because there was a phone dock and a lamp right there. The light was off and the dock empty, just like the bed.

Two guitars stood in the corner. One acoustic, the other electric. Did he play the guitar?

It was no mystery why he hadn't brought her there before. Just being around his things revealed so much of him.

She couldn't go wandering around without clothes and wouldn't call out to him like he was her butler. They'd gone through the closet on the way to the bathroom when they arrived. She went in there seeking something to wear. The first thing she snagged was a shirt. One of his, so the arm was big enough for her splint. Thank goodness. While buttoning it, she noticed…

"Is that my…?"

Women's clothes hung at the other end of the closet. Her clothes. When the hell had…? In the drawers, there was underwear, socks, all hers.

She put on a pair of her panties and forgot about looking for her sling. If they'd had time to get things from her apartment and put them in his closet, she must've been out for hours.

No wonder she was so thirsty, though even that was taking a back seat to finding her host. What had they talked about? Had she agreed to…? Were they living together? She remembered the shower, how he towel dried her whole body and moisturized her skin. Then he'd… She stopped on the threshold of the bedroom. He'd blow-dried her hair. It was surreal. That had to be a dream… didn't it? Except when she touched her locks, they were sleek. As they would be if blow-dried, rather than just left to dry as she slept.

"The thirty-eight?"

A male voice. Somewhere. Where?

There were only a dozen stairs up to the bedroom. Beneath was the living room, all open, airy. The ceiling towered above, and windows dominated the back wall. Dark furniture and metal accents made it all very industrial, very masculine, very Connel.

Male voices carried again. But from where? No one occupied the living room below.

Going down the stairs, she peeked into the perpendicular hallway. Geez, a square tunnel to another big room with an oval dining table and chairs around it.

"No," Connel said in that room. "Less than an hour… no."

Was he on the phone? She'd thought there were other voices. Someone crossed the other end of the hallway to go sit at the table.

Strat. Daly wasn't far behind.

"No," Connel again. "Make me say it again."

She shivered. Did he have to use that growly voice when her defenses were low?

Rolling on the wall, she rounded the corner to traverse the hallway.

Strat noticed her first. "Hey! Was beginning to think he'd sent you away somewhere."

She smiled. "Only to his bed," she said, going over to rest a hand on his shoulder.

Connel stood at the other side of the broad kitchen island, phone to his ear.

Daly was still on his feet. "How you doing, Ser?"

"Better," she said, arching her shoulders back. "Stiff."

"That'll be taken care of."

Connel.

She hadn't heard his call end. Maybe he'd just hung up. He only looked for a second, then went to the fridge.

"Me and the guys are around," Daly said. "Want us to pick anything up for you?"

"Front and center, Ser," Connel said. She left Strat to go over as he turned from the fridge with a glass of juice, which he put in her good hand. "Where's your pain? Gimme a number."

"I'm not sore," she said, sipping the juice. "No more than I have been since the thing."

"A number."

"Four, maybe."

"Go back to bed."

"What time is it? I feel like I've slept for a week."

"A day," Strat said, and she spun around. "It's Tuesday."

"It's Tuesday," she said, her eyes bugging at the dark wall of night beyond the far window. "But it's night."

"It's almost ten."

"The club's open."

"The club's open?" Strat said. "That's your first thought?"

Stupid. Yes. "Stag's my security," she muttered.

Her rock, the place that kept her safe. Only when she wasn't there did fear or tragedy visit.

The glide of Connel's hand up her shoulder blade under her hair loosened her tension. It came around to her throat and eased her back against him.

"Your security is here," he murmured, squeezing just a little. "Where are you always safe?"

"With you," she breathed, arousal thick in her panting tone.

How did he do that? She'd thought it was his eyes, but the pulse in her pussy begged otherwise.

Guiding her head aside, he bowed to kiss the side of her neck, right on her carotid pulse.

"So you living here now?" Daly asked.

"I didn't even know here was here," Strat said.

"You only know now because she vouches for you," Connel said, once again all business. "Fuck her over and it'll be over for you."

"Threatening my friends?" she asked. He kissed her neck again and let go to walk away. Without his contact, her body ached. She turned to the concerned Strat, still sitting at the table. "Did you talk to Lach?"

"I leave that to Im, but yeah, she has. He wants to talk to you."

"I bet he does," she said, drinking some more.

"Your cop brother know about you and the boss?" Daly asked.

"No," Connel said before she could open her mouth. "Niall's got word out to the guys. Mention her name next to mine and you're finished with me."

They'd come far from the guy threatening to broadcast their intimacy to the whole world.

"You got it, Boss."

"Go do your jobs."

She opened her mouth to stall Strat but thought better of it before she spoke. Yeah, she didn't want her friend to leave, but she also wanted to find out what was going on in Connel's head.

She drank some more juice, turning to meet Connel's eye as the other men walked away. The door closed and then… silence.

She put the juice on the counter, licking the sweetness from her lips.

"No more games?"

He sauntered closer and leaned in, planting his hands on the edge of the counter on either side of her, penning her in.

"Do you want to play games, Macushla?"

She smiled. "Tell me what that means." The corner of his lips rose as he unlocked his elbows to dip down and kiss his favorite spot above her clavicle. "Thank you for letting me sleep."

Kissing her neck, his fingers popped one of her buttons, two buttons, and kept on going. "Mm," he said in acknowledgment.

"Are there cameras here?"

"You want there to be cameras?" he asked, stooping to kiss along her collarbone and back.

When his lips brushed her pressure point, she exhaled ecstasy. "You always do that."

"Turn you on?" he asked, opening her shirt to crouch lower and kiss her breast. "You make the most incredible noises."

He boosted her onto the counter and her lips curved. "You ask me what I want. Do I want cameras? Do I want blondes?"

"The blondes don't come here."

"I don't want the blondes," she said, combing her fingers into his hair as he kissed her nipple.

"How careful do I have to be?"

"My bruises are still tender, but I know you'd never hurt me." She laughed, raising her knees to rest her calves against him. "Outside the playroom anyway."

"That's not what I was talking about," he said, rising to plant his hands on the counter again.

No, the somber demeanor he landed on her betrayed his meaning.

The answer to that question was she didn't know. What she did know? She wanted no other man close to her.

"Maybe you'll have to be patient."

Skimming his hands down her thighs, he coiled them around his hips and cradled her ass, picking her up.

Without her sling, she could rest her forearm on his shoulder and loop the other around him. "Don't you want to go to the club?"

"No."

"Why?" she asked, her fingers toying with the hair at the back of his head. "Stag's where you do business."

"Not tonight."

He carried her upstairs, back to the bed she'd left not long ago. He sat her on the edge to take the shirt from her body and pushed her hips further onto the mattress before slipping off her panties.

"Why the star treatment?" she asked, watching him undress. "Not that I'm complaining about having the McDade patriarch's undivided attention…" She smiled. "But it feels like I'm waiting for the other shoe to drop."

He shed his boxer-briefs and climbed onto the bed to brace himself over her.

"People follow my orders, or they die." As demonstrated in his basement. "They piss me off, they die. I don't like them?"

"Let me guess, they die," she said, resting her injured arm in her cleavage.

"I do what I want when I want. I don't ask permission. I don't apologize. I do things my way."

"Okay," she said, scratching her nails in his stubble. "How does that answer my question?"

"We heard the sirens before we knew about the attack."

"You think they were coming for you?"

"No. I was pissed they were on my turf 'cause I decide what happens on my turf."

"Of course," she said, her fingers finding his hair again. "And you probably sent your guys to check it out."

"When they said it was you... They call me Ire, but I'd never known such instant, visceral rage." As he hissed in a breath, he bared his teeth. "They touch my woman in McDade territory..."

Mm, his form was delicious. Hanging over her, no part of his upper body touched her. Much as she wanted skin-to-skin contact, she didn't mind his muscles working. Either way worked for her.

"I think you sent a message." Being both her attackers were already dead. "No one will start anything in McDade territory without your say so."

"I went to the hospital."

Her gaze sprang to his. "What?"

"You say I have power. I say I do things my way, but... I knew you didn't want me in there."

"You stayed away for me," she said, her fingertips learning his brow. "So my family wouldn't know about us."

"I could've marched in and taken over. I'm fucking good at being in charge."

That wasn't his only strength.

She laid a palm on his cheek. "It's not because I'm ashamed of you. I'm not embarrassed about being attracted to you, it's just… complicated."

"I didn't hear your account until later. When we found out what happened, that they targeted you for being a McDade… that you kept your mouth shut."

"I told you, they'd just have killed me." Her fingertips trailed down to his torso. "They didn't call me a McDade." As far as she remembered. "I think they knew I wasn't."

"Wasn't what?"

"A McDade."

"You sure?" Their eyes met again. "If you're not born a McDade, you join the ranks through graft or initiation. You bled for us. Showed your loyalty. You are a McDade now. Like it or not. You stood up to the other side for us. You have a target on your back now. One all McDades wear."

Which was probably why he had Daly and Strat staying so close. Manzani, Gambatto, Byrne, they all had it too. Anyone entangled in the world of organized crime wore a target recognized by the other sides.

"My McDade," she whispered.

He descended slowly, meeting her mouth with his while he kept his weight braced. She appreciated his concern for her injuries, but really wanted to feel him, on her, in her, everywhere.

Breaking the kiss, his eyes landed on hers, though their mouths were just an inch apart. "You want us to trust each other?"

"Yes," she said. "Isn't that what you want?"

"Is it what you want? I can give you everything, Cushla Machree, but you have to give all of yourself in return. This is not a life, a world, that's easy to abandon."

What did this mean? Neither of them could

know until they were in it. Yes, it was unexplored territory for her, but she had a feeling Connel didn't have a manual for it either. They were feeling their way. His actions proved his willingness to go the distance. How did she show her gratitude and faith in him?

How was she supposed to…?

Licking her lips, certainty boosted her determination. "I am your subordinate," she whispered, fixated on him. "I exist beneath you, under you." Understanding seeped into him. He recognized his words. "I don't think. Don't make decisions." She paused, hooking a hand around the back of his neck. "My life is yours. I am yours." He tilted his head to hold his lips near hers, tasting the words as she spoke them. "McDade property on your terms. Your limits. I obey. Yield. Surrender. I don't resist or get in your way."

Pressing his lips to hers, they lingered there and raised a whisper, holding just at the threshold. "What is your job?"

"My job is to support you."

"Give yourself to me, submit to me, and I'll look after you, Macushla, in a way no other man can or will."

He shot a man for invading their intimacy and killed two men for touching her. His capabilities were no joke. The life hadn't seduced her, the man had, but God knew why her connection to him was so strong. Whatever the reason, they definitely weren't done with each other yet.

TWENTY-SEVEN

PROPPED AGAINST THE pillows, she read the news on Connel's tablet. With his permission, of course. It felt like an hour since he'd left her alone in his bed.

His timing was great. She'd just finished an article when he returned. Still naked, he wasn't at all self-conscious as he brought steaming bowls over.

She loved it. Getting to see him in his incredible glory. Sculpted to perfection. Every time it thrilled her.

"Why are you smiling?" he asked, putting one bowl on the nightstand and holding the other to her as he got onto the bed at her side.

"What does this one mean?" she asked, touching the vertical line of black writing beneath his arm on his ribcage.

"Nothing without effort," he said, putting the bowl in her hand. "Eat."

"Thanks," she said, wrinkling her nose as he picked up some noodles in the chopsticks. "I haven't been in the mood for food mu—"

He forced her to take the noodles from the

wood. She was all ready to say enough until she chewed and the flavor burst in her mouth. Surprise had to be written all over her face and he was drinking in every detail.

"Oh my God," she said, swallowing. "That's really good. That's amazing."

He fed her some more. For the first time in more than a week, she wanted to eat.

"Do you want to go downstairs to the table?"

"No," she said, propping the bowl between her drawn-up knees and her chest, stealing the chopsticks from him to feed herself. "Did you cook this? I mean did you make it or did some restaurant sneak it upstairs for you? How does a guy like you…? You can cook. Play guitar. Speak two languages—"

"Three, fluently. I get by with a few more," he said and shrugged. "Makes business easier."

Humility? Not like him, which explained the swagger that lit his eye.

"Did you cook this?" she asked. "Are you messing with me?"

"Strangers don't come up here."

"How does a guy like you learn to cook like this?"

He twisted around to get the bowl from behind him. "My mom."

She stopped eating. Had she expected him to answer? Maybe. But not something so momentous in such a casual way.

"How old we're you when she passed?"

"Eight," he said, stirring his noodles. "Don't eat too fast. Your stomach needs to adjust."

"Does that mean no liquor?"

"You want a drink?"

"I like your whiskey," she admitted. "Makes me think of the first time we kissed."

Was that the comfort she got in the back of the

car all those times she looked for courage?

He leaned in to kiss her. "How much are you struggling?"

"I don't know," she said, her focus descending to the food.

"Talk to me."

He took her bowl and put both aside. When he turned back to her, she swooped in to catch his mouth with hers. They'd be okay. They'd get over it with time. If she could distract him, and herself, they wouldn't have to discuss it.

He caught her jaw to ease their mouths apart, holding it while with the other hand he combed her hair from his grip, tucking it back with the rest of her locks.

"Do you know how easy it is for me to get laid?" he murmured. "How fast I can fill my bed with pussy?" She tried to pull away, but his grip tightened, holding her there. "One phone call. One text. I can have twenty whores up here fighting over my cock." He pulled her mouth to his, kissing her hard and fast. "I've never been faithful to a woman." Again, she tried to pull away, but he hauled her back. "Never been unfaithful either. I've never committed to one. My relationships are casual. Open. I do what I wanna do when I wanna do it, and I don't answer to anyone." Letting her go, he dropped back against the propped-up pillows and slouched his hips, taking his cock in hand. "You want it, take it. I'll add you to the list of sluts on speed dial."

He had a direct way of making a point. Scooching closer, her eyes stayed on his though her hand curled around his on his cock.

To be different, to show their relationship the respect it deserved, they needed to be more than sex. For sure he could get twenty whores delivered to his loft. But he'd chosen her to join him in bed. Her alone. Because she was a random slut? No. Because she was something else. What something else? She had no clue.

If they could commit murder together, they should be able to open up to each other, right?

"Last week was sex tapes, foursomes, and riding crop punishments," she said. "You have an appetite—"

"I don't need that bullshit," he sneered. "Think I haven't had every kink under the fucking sun? Sex was nothing. I didn't even give a shit about it. Who the fuck cares when everything's on offer twenty-four seven?"

"You *didn't* give a shit?" she asked, squeezing him. "You do now?"

His fingers slid out from under hers to move over them, sliding them up and down his thick shaft.

"Fuck… you're something different," he said on a groan, his head dropping back. "Everything was new to you. Shit I take for granted… it was new to you."

"You liked that?" she asked, switching the angle of her thumb to stroke his head as her pace and strength increased. "You like this?"

Her whispered words came as she kissed his arm and wriggled lower to lick his tip. Even taking him into her mouth, the power of him overwhelmed her. Hard, broad, pulsing against her tongue, the connection to her own strength grew.

"Conn," she breathed against him, tightening her lips in a kiss to force him through into her mouth.

Another groan and his fingers fell to her hair. "Macushla."

Climbing over his leg, she settled between them to suck him deep. He didn't want to push her, didn't want her hurt, but the tangle in her hair tightened.

Slurping him from her lips, she placed short, wet kisses on his shaft.

"How many women have sucked your cock?" she asked, humming around him. He stroked her. When she blinked up, his drowsy eyes were fixed on her.

"Hmm, baby?"

Keeping her hand working, jerking, tightening and loosening, she slithered up his body, parting her legs over his hips so her pussy just kissed the beaded moisture on the head of his dick.

He squeezed her breasts. "You teasing my cock, baby?"

"You didn't want it," she purred, her lips on his.

Her hand kept going. Squeezing harder, she dropped her hips until his tip just peeked into her before angling his head to massage her clit.

"Like it risky, baby?"

Skimming his palms up her back, under her hair, one after the other, the ripple of pleasure cascaded through her as he urged her against him with the ebb and flow of his purposeful caress.

"I like getting you off," she murmured, kissing him. "I want you to come on me."

"On you or in you?"

Her body was moving in time with her hand as her muscles tired. "In my mouth?"

"In your pussy," he said, grabbing her ass in both hands. "We're clean."

"How do you know I'm clean?"

"Read your hospital records," he said, yanking her so hard that her hand got lost between them. "You have an IUD."

"I do," she breathed, kissing him one way then the other. "Do you want to be inside me, baby? You want to come in me?"

"More than you fucking know," he said, reaching up to sweep her hair from her ear and—it came back with a condom in his fingers.

How did he do that?

Disappointment came with confusion. "You don't want to be in me?"

"You don't want me hooked, baby," he said, rolling on the condom. "Take it as slow as you need."

Fondling her, he waited, jutting up between them.

"My turn to torment you?"

"Macushla gets what she wants."

Apparently not because the barrier remained between their bodies. She missed the man he'd been between their sheets in Stag. But as she slithered down onto him, satisfaction came with security. She needed to be gentle and in control. Somehow, he'd known exactly what she needed without her having a clue.

TWENTY-EIGHT

"SEE HOW FINE I am," she said to her brother over drinks that Wednesday night. "You need to stop asking. I'm fine."

"You need to answer your phone."

"I was texting you," she said. "I'm sorry, I went in to work like everything was fine and then slept through all of yesterday. I just passed out. I guess it was too much."

"You should've called last night. You need to be calling. Keeping in touch. I don't want to worry every time there's a homicide call that you're going to be the victim."

"Strat is looking out for me," she said.

"Yeah, he told Immie. I'm hearing about my baby sister via my ex-girlfriend and her father."

"You're right, I'm sorry."

"I know you're disappointed the investigation hasn't got further. Trust me, I'm on them every day. We will find everyone responsible." No, they wouldn't. "The first guy, the dead guy, we got an ID. Turns out he did business with the Manzanis but moonlighted for other crews."

"Which could've got him in trouble."

"Maybe. It's hard to narrow down the list of wise guys by your description of the second perp, but we're doing what we can. There are whispers Manzani diverted some of his people to Miami, but that's just rumor. Could include your guy or not."

"I'm trying to be focused," she said. "Positive. Aiming ahead."

"Yeah, but this won't just go away on its own. Talk to someone. Did the docs recommend a therapist or something?"

"They talked about it," she said, sipping her virgin margarita. "But it's too soon. I can't really figure out how I feel about anything. My mood is swinging back and forth."

"That's why you talk to someone. They help you figure it out."

"When I'm ready. I still need to… process."

"Don't let it fester. I've seen a lot of good cops go down that road. It's not easy to come back from there."

Was that what she was doing? She'd been present for the murder of a man and felt no regret. Would that come flooding in? Connel had been doing it for years. How did he let it roll off?

"I will talk."

"You can talk to me. About anything. If you want to talk."

She smiled. "You're a good brother."

"Yeah. Yeah. When are you back at the hospital?"

"Tomorrow," she said. "I hope I'll get my splint off. I'll still need to do exercises to build my strength, but I can do without wearing a bag in the shower."

"Have you had problems with anything? I can come over and help."

"Not in the shower you can't."

"No, I'll call Immie if you need that kind of help."

"I do not want to shower with your ex-girlfriend," she said. "We're not even friends."

"You should be. You're alike. Headstrong. Stubborn. Willful."

"Aren't those three virtually the same thing?"

"Feisty then."

"How come no one ever uses that word to describe a guy? Guys are confident. Women are apparently feisty, like they shouldn't be confident." Her hand stopped on its way to her glass. "Independent. That's another one. Men are bachelors. Carefree. Women are independent. Like that's a bad thing. No one talks about a man being independent. They're just assumed to be. Yet a woman will be described as independent as though they're opinionated wenches who should get back in the kitchen."

"Careful you don't fall off that soapbox," Lachlan said, laughing. "Who wound you up and let you go? All I said was you should hang with Immie."

"Maybe when everything's calmed down, we'll hang out. You're a one-on-one guy. You were with her or me. We didn't do things all together."

"We don't do together as a family. We're all too busy," he said. "But that should change. If anything, your assault showed us we need to be closer. We need to take the time for each other. You want to do dinner this weekend? The four of us?"

"Maybe," she said. "I may have to work."

"You should take time off."

"To stare at the walls? No, I have work to do."

Lachlan had said no one would've registered her

missing if people hadn't heard her scream. Dorsey could be out there somewhere screaming. It might have taken twenty years, but she was listening. Dorsey didn't deserve to wait a minute more.

TWENTY-NINE

"I NEED TO WRITE something," she said in the car with Strat a little while later.

"Write what?"

To go for drinks with Lachlan, it made more sense to have Strat drive her in his car. Lachlan wouldn't question that now he knew the two were friends. The Bentley wasn't far away. And the van of goons still followed. She had her own entourage. Connel wasn't taking any chances and she wouldn't argue.

"I need to talk to Conn about Dorsey. Other things keep happening. I can't keep putting it off."

"No one saw him between when we left his loft yesterday and him showing up at the club after lunch today."

"We slept in. It was a compromise. I wanted to work, and he wanted me to rest. So we stayed up late and slept in. I got to squeeze in some more research, and he got to watch me rest."

"Any luck finding Clancy?"

"Not yet. I'm hoping Conn knows where he is.

The McDades are sort of scattered all over—"

He did a double take when her words stopped dead. "What? The McDades are what?"

"We have to go to the club," she said, reaching for the dash. "Please."

"Boss said to take you back to his place."

"I know, but it's important. I'll deal with his anger if there is any. Please."

"I'll probably get in as much trouble for ignoring your order as I will not following his," Strat said, navigating a turn that would lead them in the direction of Stag. "Taking orders from a squirt who could practically be my kid."

"I don't tell you enough how I value you looking out for me."

"Wouldn't be anywhere else," he said, flashing her a consoling smile.

The club was only a few blocks away, and traffic was quiet, so they got there fast.

"I can go in alone," she said when they stopped. "Security is right there. You go park."

Plenty of cars liked to roll up to the curb and expel their glamorous occupants. She might not be glamorous, but she did want to go inside, and Strat might get in trouble for dumping the car there to go in with her.

"Okay, I'll watch," he said, resting a wrist on the top of the wheel. "Once you're inside, I'll go round back."

Security barely looked at her as she entered between them. Same guy who'd blocked her before and she wasn't supposed to be there that night. Still, apparently, she was on the list again.

Someone shouted and there was a scuffle going on, which might be why no one stood at the bottom of the office staircase. It would've pissed her off if Connel was unprotected. Thank God there were goons on the stairs again. They didn't say anything and weren't always there. She'd have to ask him what the criteria were for posting the troops.

She opened the door wondering if maybe she should've gone the other way. Except the office was empty. She closed the door, figuring they'd be upstairs.

"My princess comes to me."

Whipping around fast, she couldn't believe Evander was there. Sitting in the middle of the chesterfield with a broad smug grin on his face. Okay, so she could believe the grin, but him being there…?

"Sorta hoped we might meet here," he said, laying a hand on the couch next to him. "Come sit down."

"No," she said, going to the desk to put down her purse.

"Did he tell you we had a meeting? That why you came?"

"No," she said, going around behind the desk to the decanter to pour some fortifying whiskey. "What are you doing here?"

"We have business, me and McDade."

When she turned back, glass at her lips, Evander was on his feet, in the middle of the stag head rug. They'd had sex in that spot, her and Connel. Somehow, seeing Evander there tarnished the memory.

"And you came running," she said. "Eager to please."

"Looks like you did too. Nice of him to bring us together." She went to the closest end of the desk as she sipped her whiskey. "Getting a taste for the Irish?" From the smirk on his face, he wasn't talking about the whiskey. "I should get you some Italian wines."

"I prefer something harder," she said, resting the glass by her throat.

He came strolling over. "I can deliver on that

too."

Usually, when he got close, she got tense and nervous. But even when he stopped a foot in front of her, she didn't flinch. The challenge in his stare was playful, eager even, yet there was intrigue, familiarity.

His hand rose, she saw it coming.

Before he made contact, she spoke. "Touch me with that and he'll relieve you of it."

His lips curved. "Don't be so sure. Our deal's important."

"Not that important."

Connel.

Both she and Evander turned toward his voice. There he stood in front of the curtain, Niall at his flank.

"She's a tempting woman," Evander said with teasing mischief, his hand still close.

She couldn't see it lingering behind her, but it was definitely there.

"Anything you touch her with, you'll leave this room without."

"Might be worth it if I get to touch her with it first."

"Upstairs."

Leaving Evander, she chose to go back around behind the desk to head for the curtain. She didn't intend to look at Connel, to distract him from pinning Evander under that intense glare. Lucky guy.

But her lover's arm came across her body, stalling her at his side.

His attention arced down to her. What did he want to say? To ask? Was he worried? Indifferent? Was this the same man who'd fed and cared for her?

Offering the glass to him, he freed her hand when he took it, allowing her to curve a hand around the back of his neck to pull him down.

Did he want to mark her in front of Evander?

Maybe. But as their lips met, a surge of need tightened her grip. She needed to mark herself in front of Evander. It might not make sense, but she'd never had this before. Never been involved with anyone she didn't fear Evander taking down.

Connel swept her hair from her face, cradling the side of her head to angle it for a deeper connection. Yet it was him, when their tongues touched, who parted their lips.

"You like anything you're wearing…" he growled.

Her smile came with the whisper of a laugh. "I'll lose it."

"Good girl," he said, his hand dropping from her head to squeeze her ass as she walked past Niall and through the curtain he held for her.

"What is it about her that gets guys by the balls?" Evander asked.

Halfway up the stairs, she crouched to sit and listen.

"We're here for business."

"You brought her here. Put her between us."

"Sersha comes and goes as she pleases."

"Believe me, I know. She's wild. Does whatever she wants."

"You talk like you know her," that from Niall.

"I've known her since she was fresh," Evander said. "Barely legal." Nineteen, but okay. "She's her own woman." Warmth and lust tainted his words. "You can't trust her. No guy can."

"You can't trust her," Connel stated.

Evander laughed. "But you can? No, you don't understand her. You think you have her loyalty? That she understands this. She doesn't understand it. If she did, you think she'd talk to us the way she does? You think she'd follow your orders like the fifty other bitches you've got lined up waiting for your cock? No, man. No."

"Your information checks out."

"She doesn't get that guys like us are capable, lethal, that we don't have limits. We could snap her in half. In a second. No one would ever find the body. Not like we haven't done it before."

"We're done talking about Sersha," Connel said, finality in his words.

"'Cause you know I'm right. She doesn't know we've tortured guys, murdered them. That we do it every day. She doesn't get we'd give up anything for our families. For the fucking privilege of our names."

"And our deal?" Connel asked as a door closed. "Where does that fit into your privilege?"

That door… Did someone leave the office or join them?

"I'm doing what needs to be done," Evander said, on the defensive. "For my family. I'm willing to make this sacrifice. To go this far."

"I'm doing it for profit."

"And that's what you value more than anything else?" Evander asked. "More than your name?"

"There's nothing I value more than my name."

"We've been on opposite sides a long time. We need a show of trust." That tone from Evander was never good. "I'm putting a lot of faith in you."

"You need me. You can't pull it off without me."

"Yeah, and you could fuck me at the first chance."

"Aye."

She shivered.

"I have all the risk," Evander said. "I'm trusting your honor… I need a show you mean this. That you're in and not just out to fuck me." In the following silence, she held her breath. "Any place you choose. Drop her off with me Friday night. I'll bring her back to you Monday morning."

Simple as that. He reduced her to a clause in a contract.

"Manzani—"

"I'll come back Friday for your answer. Don't put her away wet… I'll do that for you."

The door closed, then something crashed so loud, she jumped. He was mad. But was he alone? Could she go to him?

"Macushla."

The quiet word prompted her to descend the stairs and slip off her shoes at the bottom before going through the curtain.

He turned his chair her way, and she went to him. He caught her wrist to pull her onto his thigh, her legs in the vee of his.

"How did you know I was there?" she asked.

Hooking a forearm under her knees, he drew them up to drape her legs across the arm of his chair and tipped her back over the other to kiss her breast.

He sucked on her, licked, kissed, his hand flattened on her flesh and slid upward to unhook her sling from the back of her neck. That allowed him to slide the strap of her dress from her shoulder to free her breast from the fabric.

Once his mouth was occupied by her nipple, his hand snaked under her skirt.

"I came here to tell you something," she said, her head falling back, her fingers twining in his hair. As his fingertips found her clit, he massaged her through her panties. "Take me home, baby."

It was getting harder to think. Breathing shallowed like a weight compressed her chest.

He sucked his mouth free of her nipple. "Doyle's on his way," he murmured, exposing her other breast, pushing against her flesh, massaging her with drowsy delight.

"I don't know who Doyle is," she said, catching his hand to guide it back down to her pussy.

"You got needs, baby?"

"I'd prefer your cock," she said, smiling as she raised her hips against his hand. "Can I have your cock?" As her ass moved, his prominent arousal beneath her made itself known. "He wants me."

"Hard not to," he said, picking her up to dump her on the desk. "Want it hard and fast? I don't have a lot of time."

Wrapping her legs around him, she used his strength to pull herself against him. "I'll take it any way you give it, baby."

Wriggling and writhing, she panted every breath. Heat and need drove her, making it impossible to be still.

He planted a hand on the desk and unbuckled his belt with the other, freeing himself before snagging a condom from the top drawer and pushing into her. All of him, long, hard, thick. Mmm, the overwhelming pressure forced its way deep. Biting her lip, she held in a yelp, but a moan escaped.

"Macushla," he growled.

"You feel so good," she murmured, arching toward him. "Fuck me, Conn."

He snatched her hips to pull her to him on every thrust. "How the fuck…" he snapped, "how the fuck do you do this to me?"

"Yes," she hissed. "Yes. Yes!" Friction and motion seared her hormones. Breathe. "Conn? Conn!" He slapped her breast and her eyes opened. "Shit."

Orgasm slammed into her and she grabbed for him, her muscles contracting, pulling him into her, fighting every withdrawal.

She didn't shout, didn't make a sound, simply

opened her mouth in a silent scream then snapped it shut, clenching her teeth hard as she rode the pleasure all the way to his climax.

"Ser. Fuck."

All of her energy went to breathing when they were both spent. He didn't withdraw even as he softened within her. That was fine, she liked him there.

"Would you do it?" he asked. Evander. That was where his head was? "If I ordered you to do it?"

"I don't have to answer that," she said, taking his hand from her breast to kiss his palm and rub her face against it. "You will never give that order."

His eyes narrowed. "How do you know?"

"Where am I always safe?" Usually he was the one asking, and she didn't wait for an answer. "You take care of me," she said, returning his hand to her breast, squeezing his fingers around her. "You take care of my body, my mind, my soul, all of me. My well-being means something to you." For whatever reason. "I've never had a man take such good care of me." Clenching her abs, she sat up. "And it's my job to support you."

"What did you come to tell me?"

She gasped. "Yes! I went for a drink with Lachlan."

He withdrew, tossing the condom in the trash before fastening his pants. "I know. I gave you permission to go." She smiled because that was true. "I track you everywhere you go." Hence how they'd found her phone. "I protect you."

"Yes, you do," she said, sliding off the desk, righting the straps of her dress to cover her breasts again. "And the McDades, which is why I wanted to tell you…"

"Tell me what?" he asked, going to the decanter to pour liquor.

"Lach said they had an ID for the first guy. Whatever, we knew that." She sat on the desk again, resting her feet in his chair. "He said they were struggling with guy two."

He replaced the stopper while drinking the liquid. "And?"

"He said it was possible guy two left," she said as he came back over.

"Left where?" he asked, handing her the glass.

"The state." The liquor burned a familiar path in her gullet. "He said Silvio Manzani sent some of his guys to Miami."

His brow reacted. "Miami? Why?"

"I don't know. But I figured if Manzanis are going to be in your cousins' neighborhood, you'd want to let them know."

He caught her chin to raise it up. "We'll go home when Doyle leaves."

"I don't mind if we stay here, provided you come to bed with me at some point. When I wake up without you, I'm lonely."

"Yeah, and horny."

"That too," she said and laughed. As he turned, she put down the glass and snagged his buckle. "Can I ask you a business question?"

"You want to know why Vex was here."

"Well, yeah, but my business, not your business." He frowned. "Can I interview you about Dorsey?"

"No," he said. "Not for your paper. Don't print it and I'll tell you everything I know."

"Why can't I print it? If there's a chance—"

"You print it, they kill her."

Shock didn't begin to... she stopped breathing and just...

"She's alive?" she managed eventually.

"Aye."

"Oh my God, she's alive! And you know she's alive? How do you know?"

"We get proof of life every few months. I get proof of life. Clancy can't look at her anymore."

"You know where your uncle is?"

"Aye," he said and tightened his grip. "What did you say to me after I told you where to find the Russian dolls?"

"You know things," she exhaled.

"I know things." They stared for just a second before the door opened. "Upstairs."

She pounced off the desk, keeping quiet and small as a stream of well-built guys entered. This time, she didn't loiter on the stairs and ascended to go to the bar.

Dorsey was alive. All this time, he knew… they needed to have a conversation. Fast.

THIRTY

SHOCKS OF PLEASURE still shimmered through her. Spasms of delight shook her as her heart slowed. In bed next to Connel, at the club, sweat clung to her skin. Sated need was impossible to comprehend. She'd never been so sexually satisfied and desperate at the same time.

In the darkness, her awareness was still hazy when he kissed her quick then jumped out of bed.

"Were you thinking of her the whole time?" he called from the closet.

She smiled and rolled onto her side, propping her head on a hand. "No worse than you thinking about Evander while we were doing it on the desk earlier."

He reappeared, frowning; he was always frowning. "You're the only thing in my head when we're fucking."

He retreated.

She sank onto her back. "We should stop having so much sex." Her smile grew again. "You're ruining me for other men."

"What time is your hospital appointment

tomorrow?"

Today more like, it was somewhere in the early hours. These times with Connel were fast becoming her favorite. When they were alone. In the dark. In bed.

"Two," she said. "Strat will take me. Lach will probably show up… They like him over at the hospital. Nurses like him."

"Women like authority," he said, joining her again, returning to their bed.

"Do they?" she asked, her fingertips meeting his cheek when he loomed over her. "They say women go for men like their fathers."

His reaction to that statement was nothing like Strat's.

"How's that working out for you?" he asked and kissed her slow before dropping onto his back beside her.

"I guess it is the authority," she said. "My grandfather, my dad, they were always the most powerful men in whatever room we were in." The way he shifted his head brought her onto her side again, this time her hand tucked under the pillow. He often did this, just lay there, head in his pillow, gaze on her or the ceiling. "What?"

Because she could see a question behind his scrutiny.

"He ever hit you?"

"My dad?" she asked, almost laughing. "God, no. He'd have to acknowledge me to hit me. Him and Lach on the other hand…"

"They fought?"

"Lachlan's so desperate for his approval, he'd beat his own ass before Dad ever got close. Did I tell you about the weird conversation I had with him?"

"With who?"

"My dad. It was the day before the… thing."

"The attack. You were attacked. Targeted and assaulted. It didn't just roll off if you still can't call it what it is."

"That's for later," she said, wriggling closer to rest her splinted arm on his chest. "Lach got me into the police records department."

Interesting slow blink of his emerald eyes. "Think of all the evidence you could destroy with access like that."

He wasn't smiling, but she laughed. "It's the records room, not the evidence locker."

"A lot of statements aren't copied to other places. If it's old enough, it's not digitized. They leave tapes in files, video and audio."

"Do you want me to destroy evidence for you?"

His head shifted so their eyes met again. "Would you?"

Free and easy felt so good.

She wasn't concerned and rose to kiss him. "I could go to prison for a long time."

"Not if we grease the right people… What did you say about waiting twenty-five to life…?" Leaving that lingering, his sincerity could go either way. "Tell me about the conversation with your dad."

"I was leaving Records and he caught me in a stairwell."

"Caught you?"

"We met," she said. "Lachlan told him I was there. It was strange, really strange. He seemed… stressed. And my dad is never stressed."

"What did he want?"

"He started by asking me to dinner, which straight away is strange because we'd already had lunch less than a week before. I can go a month without hearing from my father. Two meals in one week? Never happens."

"I thought he'd be more on you after the attack," he said. "That he'd have squads dedicated to your protection. Superintendent's daughter, alderman's granddaughter, he could justify it."

"I don't doubt Lachlan thought about it," she said, rising to slide a leg over him, straddling his torso. "I'm happier you're doing it." His nuance was subtle, but that drew his curiosity. "More sex this way."

Bowing over him, their lips found each other again. "Dunno, bet there's a lot of boys in blue desperate to nail the boss's daughter."

"I have dated cops," she said, her fingers trailing down him as she sat up again. "A lot of cops."

"I bet you have."

"Trouble with guys like that, I never know if they're interested in me, or getting close to the men in my family."

"There's always an ulterior motive," he said, cupping her breasts. "There's power in having influence."

"Lachlan's too good to be manipulated like that. Though I know he feeds his ex information from time to time. He trusts her. Still loves her, I think."

"With you. You have influence."

"I don't. I suppose people could think that, but it's really not true. Any guy might believe I could whisper in my father or grandfather's ear for them." She exhaled a laugh. "Boy, would that guy be disappointed."

"You're his daughter. You don't think he'd do whatever it took to keep you safe?"

"I think his concern is the integrity of the institution. Something he drummed into Lachlan over and over, all his life. In the hospital last week, he was pissed Lachlan wanted to be part of the investigation."

"To get a conviction, the process has to be airtight. Chain of custody, ethical boundaries, all that shit."

"I guess," she said, her forefingers caressing the furrows of his ridged body. "It's enviable how my father can be clear-headed and detached all the time. Every time I react with emotion, he gets so pissed off."

"He lives with rules. Expectation. There's a lot on his shoulders."

Her lips curled again and she planted a hand on his chest. "Are you defending my father? The superintendent? You? Mr. *Ire* McDade?"

Connel didn't seem to find it funny. "You don't even realize it."

Her smile faded when he responded with such solemnity. "I don't realize what?"

"We've killed together, Macushla," he said, his hand sliding over hers. "I don't give a shit about the superintendent. Honestly, couldn't give a crap. The guy doesn't enter my head."

"Okay, you want me to stop talking?" she asked, figuring he was done listening to her bullshit. Climbing off him, she tried to lie down, but he still held her hand on his chest. "There's no reason you should give a—"

He yanked her hand, jerking her to him so hard, she gasped as her body, injured arm and all, collided with his.

"You think you react with emotion? Baby, you haven't met me," he snarled. "I defend the cunt who hurt you or I kill him. Choose your poison."

"The cu… my father? You'd kill my father?" she whispered, stunned and… awed.

"If you asked me to."

"You'd kill if I asked you to?"

"You follow my orders, Macushla. Whatever I tell you to do, you do."

But that didn't work the other way, did it? Unless she told him something was utmost for her well-being.

She couldn't imagine him ever resisting anything that would assure her welfare.

Like every part of her was a tingling, exposed nerve, his words vibrated everywhere. They'd had sex, but it didn't matter, she could feel herself growing slick for him again.

"It's seductive," she murmured. "Your world. Being a part of it. I didn't realize before that I… it's exciting and terrifying. I've done things with you, I… I'm not scared of it. Why am I not scared of it?"

"Where are you always safe?"

"With you," she said.

It could only be him. Had to be him. She hadn't felt that way with Evander. She didn't fear Connel or his world; their connection was true. Instinct. Out of the stratosphere compared to anything she'd experienced with the man they called Vex.

"Do you believe that when you say it?"

"Yes," she said, losing herself in him. "I always feel safe with you." And she didn't fear him. Maybe she'd have lounged there in that reality a little longer, if it wasn't for the conversation with her father intruding. When she sat up, he let her hand move back to his torso. "They know you're colluding with councilmen. He wanted their names. My father wanted to know if I had access."

"To me?"

"I told him he did a lot of talking about doing the right thing. That it wasn't the right thing to abuse someone's trust. I told him it was unethical and went against my professional integrity to discuss anything I saw or heard in relation to my work. I told him it wasn't my responsibility to tie bows for the cops." Her attention floated away. "I forgot all about… I guess that's why he was still pissed in the hospital." A whisper of a laugh crossed her lips. "He said I'd always be protected in this city. Then the next day, I…" Sinking down, she nestled against him, resting her head on his shoulder, by his stag head tattoo. His arm curled around to lose his fingers in her hair. "He said if I withheld, I was an accessory."

His digits clenched. "He threatened you?"

"I don't think he meant it like that. He was just trying to scare me. I called him paranoid… It's ridiculous, right?" she said, turning her lips against his skin. "He wants the names of city officials I've seen you interact with and I refuse to cooperate, but I tell you every detail of my conversation with him. Maybe he didn't raise me so smart after all."

His fingers spread a little more against her scalp, massaging his entitlement into her. She closed her eyes, appreciating his warmth and acceptance.

"Sonofabitch," he murmured.

Her eyes opened. "What are you—"

"Shit," he said and got up, forcing her to move aside.

"What?" she asked as he picked up his cellphone from the nightstand. "What is it?" He dialed. "Baby?"

"I don't want you alone with him," he said as he raised the phone to his ear.

"Alone with who?"

"Your father," he said, then raised the microphone. "One second…" His eyes widened as they met hers. "Macushla? Acknowledge my order."

"Yes, okay," she said, still flummoxed. "I won't be alone with him."

He raised the phone and started for the doorway. "They've got the superintendent."

The words hit her as he exited. Got the… she didn't know who he was talking to, but what he'd just said implied…

He returned to go into the closet where his voice rose. "…at the club… We didn't get that far… Aye…"

She got up to peek inside at him. "Conn?"

Now wearing underwear, he opened an arm her way, phone still at his ear. "As soon as…" She went into his proffered semi-embrace, and he pulled her against him. "Do it… Aye… Bet your fucking life." He hung up and tossed the phone onto the vanity. Taking her upper arms, he parted their bodies to make eye contact. "Daly's gonna take you back to the loft."

"I don't want to go back to the loft," she said. "Are you coming with me?"

He snagged one of his shirts to feed her arms into it. "I've got business."

"Business at three in the morning?" she asked. "What did you mean they have the superintendent? Who has him?"

He exhaled and snagged her hand to lead her out of the closet and seat them on the edge of the bed.

"What did the guys we killed want?" he asked, catching her hair between his fingers as he scooped his large hand around the side of her head.

"They wanted to know who was on your payroll." She searched her memory. "Who you were greasing." Her attention leaped to his. "Who's McDade got on the council?" His expression relaxed enough to agree with the conclusion she was reaching on her own. "They wanted the same information my dad wanted."

"When your father didn't get it the easy way, Silvio Manzani sent his guys in to get it the hard way."

She couldn't even think, it was… unfathomable. Her chest tightened; sickness constricted her throat.

"No," she said, her head moving in a loose shake. "No, but that means…" Her ears rang. "My father wouldn't."

"People are complicated, Macushla."

"No," she said, trying to focus. Her father would… he wouldn't. How could he get mixed up with someone like Silvio Manzani? "Does he have something on him?"

"Maybe," he said. "Or your father's like every other sap out there." She sought an explanation. "Pussy or green, baby. Only two reasons a guy does anything."

And family. At least he was nice enough not to add that one. If her father was in cahoots with the Manzanis, it wasn't for the sake of their McLeod family.

"Maybe he wants evidence," she said. "Maybe law enforcement knows you've paid people off and he wants to bring them to justice."

"You wanna talk to him? Ask him what's going on?"

Did she? Would he be honest with her? "I have to talk to Lach."

He pulled her a little closer. "You put this on him, baby, he'll do what any man would do and confront your father. If it's true, he'll pursue him."

Would Lachlan arrest their father? Was that even possible? How could she put her brother in that position? And if they were wrong…

"This is about the Harvest deal?"

"Yeah."

"What is the Harvest deal?"

"Over at the old Harvest site by the river, there's a complex of empty buildings. We want it."

"The city owns it?" she asked.

He nodded. "And we need the area rezoned."

"You need votes and willing officials," she said. "What does that have to do with Manzani?"

"Where is the Harvest site? Geographically?"

It struck her fast. "The border of McDade and Manzani territory."

The Gambatto buffer was dwindling by the day.

"Aye."

"They want it too?"

"Stopping us from getting control of the region is their priority. And that means taking it from us. It's all haggling, baby, who has more, who has less."

"So they have people in their pockets who will jockey for them." But she didn't get it. "My father doesn't vote on council meetings. He isn't involved in zoning decisions."

"Bet a lot of guys in that building owe him. New guys want to impress him. You said he has power."

"Yeah, but not like my grandfather… Oh, God…"

"I don't know about the old man," he said. "Approaching him is a risky move."

"He's never taken a payoff?"

"Not from me."

Sense was returning, though incredulity took its place. "Can we consider my father might be acting under duress? Maybe he's a victim, under pressure."

His touch descended until his thumb ran across her lower lip. "Either way, he's feeding Manzani."

Grief was weighty. "We can't trust him." He caressed her face while she gathered the courage to ask, "Did he know?" Biting into her lip, she fought to dam the tears. "Did he… that Manzani sent his guys to me?"

For a second, he said nothing, just watched the lip she worried. "You want to stick to our honesty kick?" Was she ready for the potential answer? Either way, she nodded. "I can lie to you, baby. I'm good at it."

"Conn," she begged.

"If I find out he knew Manzani's plan to target you, don't ever leave me alone with him," he said. "Only one of us will come out alive."

It wasn't a yes. Wasn't a no.

"Boss?"

Though she was the one with her back to the doorway, Connel closed the open shirt over her body.

"In a minute," he called to his guy. "You wanna stay here, Macushla?"

Feeling like that. Dirty. Used. Betrayed? No, she didn't want to stay there. She wanted to go to her dad to demand the truth. Would the answer make her feel better? If he was in trouble, maybe they could help. If not, and she found out he'd known about the attack in advance… She'd be sick. And then what? He was in charge of the police. Why would anyone believe her over him?

"I've gotta go talk to the guys."

"Wait," she said, catching his hand before it could go anywhere. "Wait, baby…"

She guided his hand to her breast as she pushed up to press her mouth to his.

Squeezing her, he caught the back of her head to force her mouth closer. His tongue went deep, giving her a taste of that security she craved.

He gripped her hair to release that shared pressure, though their lips stayed whisper close.

"You're a McDade," he growled. "You're gonna be okay. You're a McDade. Tell me."

"I'm a McDade."

He kissed her fast. "Lay down and I'll be back later. Want a pill? Something to help you sleep?"

"No," she murmured, laying a hand on his chest. "You'll stay close?"

"I'm not going anywhere," he said, increasing his pull to ease her further back. "This is your kingdom."

"Act like it," she whispered. "I'm a McDade."

"You're a McDade," he said and kissed her quick. "Stay here."

He got up and left. She stared into nothing for some length of time, then sank forward to bury her face in Connel's pillow.

Her father corrupt? It was the Twilight Zone. He

couldn't have known she'd be hurt. He couldn't. No, they hadn't always had the best relationship, but he wasn't callous. Pussy or green. Would they motivate her father? Maybe if he wasn't the man she thought he was. Either he was in serious trouble, or she'd been duped her whole life.

THIRTY-ONE

GOING THROUGH THE office and down the stairs, she was grateful for the insulated mug she'd found in the kitchen. Coffee was her lifeblood, and Connel's coffee was the best she'd ever tasted. Maybe she was biased. Everything there, around him, was better than anywhere else.

There were people at the foot of the stairs. Unusual for that time of day. Better than finding the place abandoned as she had when waking up alone in the past.

The broad guy taking up the full doorway moved aside when she got to the bottom.

Strat came into view. "Is it true?" he asked, getting in front of her when she stepped off the stairs.

Not like she had to ask what he was talking about. Oddly, it was reassuring she wasn't the only one blindsided by the possibility of her father's duplicity.

"I don't know," she said, righting her purse under her arm. "I think so."

"I can't fucking believe it. Always thought he was

straight as an arrow."

He and her both. "People are complicated."

Sidestepping, he stayed in her way. "Are you gonna talk to him?"

"No. I mean what's he going to say?" Not like her father ever felt the need to justify himself to her. "I don't want to make him desperate." She tried to pass him again and he got in her path. "What are you—why won't you let me leave?"

"'Cause I told them not to." Connel's voice echoed along the corridor, attracting everyone's attention. "Give Strat the purse and coffee." She did. "Come here."

She went down the corridor to where he opened a door and went inside. The coat check. She'd never been in there before. Empty racks with hangers lined up for what seemed like miles.

With a hand on her waist, he urged her back against the wall. "You woke up lonely."

"I did," she said, giving him her complete focus. "But it's okay, I know you're busy."

"Text me today."

"When?"

"Whenever you go anywhere."

"Thought you tracked me," she said, tucking her fingers behind his buckle inside his waistband.

"Yeah, but I want you to choose to submit. Every detail."

She smiled because she'd given him that insight into himself. "I'll text."

"I want a full report of what they say at the hospital."

"Okay. I'll record the audio."

"I have an event here tonight."

"I can stay at my place or over at Strat's, it's fine," she said, using her grip on him to boost higher. "Kiss me goodbye."

"I kiss you now, we're going upstairs," he said, the back of his fingers floating up her cheek. "I want you here tonight, before midnight."

Oh, unexpected. "If you want me here—"

"I want easy access."

"Easy access to…" His forearm landed on the wall above her head. As it slid upward, he loomed closer. "What kind of event is this?"

"You know you drive men wild?" he said under his breath, fixating on her mouth.

"I do? No, I don't."

"The sway in those fucking hips when you walk. That smile you land on us, that naughty light in your eyes."

What a tease. "Thought you didn't want to go upstairs," she said, freeing her hand and twisting it around to slide it south, massaging him through his pants. "So why are you seducing me?"

"Is that what I'm doing?" he asked, gathering her skirt in his fist. "Being in you clears a guy's head."

"You need your head cleared, baby?"

"Gotta do without your pussy all day."

A laugh left her lips. "It's easier to work when you know it's upstairs waiting?"

"Open all hours."

"For you," she said, opening his pants to slip her hand inside.

"Wall or floor?"

"Do me on the counter," she said, draping her arms around his neck. Foregoing the sling had been a good decision. "Every time I walk by, I'll think of you."

He picked her up to carry her around to the counter. The closed shutter concealed them from the hallway. The metal wasn't exactly military grade, and the guys out there had ears, but that wouldn't stop them. As he rolled on the condom, she wriggled out of her panties. She'd woken up lonely, but definitely wasn't alone.

THIRTY-TWO

"I SHOULD GIVE you gas money," she said to Strat in the driving seat. "You're quiet this morning."

"Didn't think I'd ever hear you like that," he said, his lips curling. "The boss makes you happy, huh?"

"We both need the distraction right now."

"I guess you came into each other's lives at the right time…" She was still trying to decipher the undercurrent when her friend spoke again. "Don't let yourself be manipulated, Scamp."

"Who's manipulating me?"

"I don't know. Your father maybe. Your boyfriend… you've known your daddy and his rules your whole life. Don't give up on him 'cause the guy of the minute doubts him."

"I asked Conn not to write him off. You've got to admit it would be a helluva coincidence, my father wants the same information I'm beaten for a day later."

"You think your father would let that happen? Your dad's an asshole. I get that. But no father would stand by and do nothing while that happened to his daughter."

The lens of experience tainted perspectives. Despite their differences, Strat was a father, just like hers, with a son and a daughter. Unlike hers, Strat valued his children, loved them the way they were. No matter what, Strat would go to war for his little girl. Nothing would get in the way of him protecting her. Whether her own father was the same on that score remained to be seen.

Still, her dad deserved the benefit of the doubt. "I don't know that he knew." About the attack, as Connel called it. Why couldn't she see it that clearly? "There are a lot of unknowns."

"Think they have something on him?"

"Maybe."

"You going to talk to the cop about it?"

"Lachlan?" In any other circumstance, he'd be who she went to for clarity and logic. Not this time. "What good would it do? I would love to get his take. But if I put it on him, he'll see it as his responsibility to find out the truth."

"It is his responsibility. He's a cop. Cops investigate shit."

"Their own fathers? The man they've worshipped their whole lives? It'll break him if it's true. Just demolish him."

"And you don't think it will come out eventually? I don't know about this deal they've got going on—"

"It's under control," she said. "Someone will win, Conn will win."

"And then what? Your father walks away clean?" His snicker was dubious. "Sorry to tell you, Scamp, shit don't work like that. If your father's on the hook, he's on the hook until he goes to jail or dies. Guys like Connel McDade don't give up an asset for free."

"Connel doesn't have my dad on the hook."

"So Manzani? You think that's any better? This

Harvest deal, whatever it is, not even the guys on the ground know the details. It's been kept close at the highest levels. They could be planning anything. It could be an attack, a robbery, whatever it is, you don't want to get involved. You want to steer clear, just in case."

"I know what it is," she said, noting Strat's double take from the corner of her eye.

"You know—he told you about Harvest?"

"I don't know every detail, but, yeah, I know what it is. Why it's causing so much acrimony."

"Okay, you've gotta help me out."

"Help you how?"

"Ire McDade doesn't do relationships, commitment. His encounters with women are business or pleasure. He fucks a woman 'cause he needs something from her or she's so hot, he wants to know he can."

"All he has to do is pick and point."

"Right," he said. "In the hospital you tell me you're through with him, then you're in his loft, and having sex with him ten feet from twenty of his guys."

"It was more than ten feet… and there weren't twenty guys."

"There were guys in the club, or didn't you know that?" he asked. "Quit changing the subject. Are you together? 'Cause Ire McDade doesn't do exclusive. He just doesn't."

"He's been clear about that."

"And you're okay with it? You know you have to be exclusive, though, right? Ire McDade would own any guy who thought about touching what he considers his property… Are you his property?"

"You don't have to worry about me. It's not like I have stacks of time to go around picking up men."

"You have more clothes at Ire's places than you do in your own apartment. Whatever's going on between you, it's screwing with his guys' heads. They've never witnessed anything like it."

"And you think his attentiveness is a ploy? That he's manipulating me?"

"Maybe," Strat said and paused a score of seconds. "Are you in love with him?"

Was she? That was a question she quashed any time it threatened to creep in.

"Can we stop at that bakery place you like? I want to get cupcakes for Steeple."

"Don't do it, Scamp," he said with severe gravity in the warning. "You fall for him and it's over. Damn whatever your father's mixed up in, you'll get sucked into a world that won't let you go."

"You don't think I'm already in it? Conn told me I had to be sure, that his world wasn't an easy one to leave. He's looking out for me."

"Guys like him look out for family. He's turning up the heat and you don't even realize it."

"So I should be suspicious of Conn? The day after I learn to be suspicious of my dad? Who am I supposed to trust?"

"You," he said. "You're learning that lesson late if you're just learning it now."

"You can't believe that. That you can only trust yourself? You don't want your kids to trust you? You didn't raise them to trust you?"

"My son trusts two people in this world, himself and Jagger Dunn."

"Not his sister?"

"Ford looks after his kid sister. He's smarter than her. Street smarter, not book smarter. Immie's got us all beat on that."

"Who does Imogen trust?"

"The cop, probably," he said. "She never forgave me for letting her go with her mother. I lost my baby girl's trust a long time ago."

"You stick to trusting you? You don't trust anyone else? No one?"

He showed her a smile. "If you weren't so corruptible, I'd trust you."

"Corruptible? You think I'm corruptible?"

"Hey, if it turns out your daddy's dirty, least you can say it's in the genes."

"I can't believe that. Just one look at Lachlan tells you our genes are good."

"Don't be so sure," Strat said. "My Immie's pure, she's all her mom. Sometimes one parent gives their all to one kid."

"My dad says I'm all my mom… Not so sure that's a good thing though."

"You remember her?"

"Sometimes I think I do… I don't know if it's memories or Lach's talk putting pictures in my head."

"You worship your brother."

"What's wrong with that?"

"You put him on a pedestal, he's bound to fall off."

"Lachlan's got good balance. I believe in him."

"Except you're in trouble, and you're not going to him."

Not because she didn't trust him to listen or support her. No doubt, if she started talking, he'd try to justify or come up with other plausible scenarios. But she knew him. Once the notion was in there, that it was even just remotely possible, he'd ask questions, and not just of her. Either he'd ruin his relationship with his father, that he valued so much, or, like Strat said, he'd have to see the man he worshipped slip from his pedestal.

"Why are you doing this?" she asked. "Trying to make me doubt everyone?"

"I want you to be safe. I don't want to see you

get hurt."

"You think Conn is going to hurt me? Or my dad?"

"Honestly, Scamp? I think they all will."

"All?" she asked.

They stopped.

The bakery. Cupcakes. Right where she'd asked him to take her.

With everything else going on, maybe it wasn't a cupcake day. But she needed a peace offering for Steeple, something to distract him from asking all the right questions.

Cupcakes were as good a chance as any.

***

CUPCAKES did their job improving Steeple's mood. On distracting him? Not so much. He'd got where he was by following the story. No amount of baked goods could change the fiber of the man. Unfortunately.

"No, Dorsey's a dead end," she said, sitting in Steeple's office like it was any other day.

"Really?" her boss asked, pulling himself in further at the desk. "How'd you figure?"

"The cops couldn't find anything. The McDades either. The girl's probably dead."

"You don't think it's worth checking it out?"

"There's nothing to find."

"Get into the investigation. Put pressure on the blues."

"Like that's easy."

"You've never shied from it before. What's your plan of action?" he asked. "What's your next lead? Are you giving up on the McDades? Where's your guard today?"

Last thing she wanted to be was the story. The

line she walked was precarious. Yes, she wanted her boss to believe she was capable and committed, but her job and reputation weren't more important than an innocent woman's life.

"My guard is around," she said, having left Strat by the elevator. "I'm not giving up on the McDades, but they're on the back burner." She took a breath. "My piece on the Manzanis was abstract. From the outside looking in. Conjecture, you know? Facts were researched, questions asked and answered. I want to go deeper."

"Deeper?"

"Ask the questions people are afraid to ask. Did you know I started writing to Helios Manzani in the course of my last article?"

"Yeah, you told me."

"I was thinking maybe I could go see him. Talk to him."

Concern weighed his expression. "About?"

"His family. How he ended up in prison."

"Murder. That's why he's in prison. For killing someone. Mystery solved."

Not by a long shot. "A lot of people in his line of work could be accused of the same. How did they get him?"

"Did you read his police file?"

"Not yet," she said. "I'll talk to Lachlan. What do you think? An exposé on the Manzanis from the one who's been off the street for years."

"An exposé on the Manzani locked up as a teenager?"

"Could he be purer than the other Manzanis?"

"Safe to say he got himself in trouble in the joint."

"Yeah, worse than his brothers?"

"Vex's got his own rep. Hell is in prison. Fury's

long gone."

Dead probably. Fury, also known as Atlas Manzani, was unaccounted for. Not missing, just location unknown.

"We start with the eldest," she said. "The forgotten Manzani. I bet he wants his story told."

"If his ego is anything like Evander's…" Steeple said. "You'll get Silvio's attention." Again. "If the Manzanis are already gunning for you…?"

"Duck and cover won't change that. I'm already on Silvio's radar. You don't win against families like that by running and hiding."

"You're going on the offensive. Taking the Manzanis on alone?"

"It's a balancing act," she said. "Maybe they won't realize I'm turning up the heat." Leaving the chair, she started for the door, glancing back at her boss. "Besides, no one said I was alone."

THIRTY-THREE

EXERCISES. Pain meds. But the splint was off. Thank God. The bruises weren't gone and her muscles still ached, but it was all progress. Every minute was progress.

As promised, she'd kept Connel up to date by text and sent him the audio of her appointment. He was up on her location all day. Right up to the point he'd requested her company.

Then she screwed up by going to her apartment for a dress and sitting down to collate her internet printouts. Somehow, she'd fallen asleep only to be awoken by her cellphone after eleven when Daly panicked something was wrong. He'd been waiting at the curb to pick her up for more than an hour.

After running around, getting ready as fast as possible, she'd jumped into the car. They were cutting it close, maybe too close. What if she arrived after midnight? What happened at pumpkin time?

Connel didn't usually give her deadlines. Something about that night had to be different.

Which she discovered on rushing into his office

to immediately be faced with breasts. Naked breasts. As they turned away, they revealed another pair beside them. She'd never seen the office so crowded. Women, all naked, completely naked, of every variation, all fawning over the sporadic men dotted around the room. There had to be four women for every guy. She wasn't even sure where to look or what was going on.

Still bug-eyed, she squeezed her way through the people, feeling rather conspicuous in her strapless ombre dress.

Seeking Connel at the desk was sort of a shot in the dark. Finding him there was a relief. Less welcome was the naked woman in his lap and the one behind the chair massaging his shoulders. With his concentration on the couple of men he was talking to, he didn't pay much notice to the three women on their knees fawning over him.

His lips moved until he spotted her. She smiled and stopped, but his head moved just a fraction to the side, the way it did when he wanted her closer. His conversation with the men forgotten, he said something to the woman in his lap. She pouted and got up to strut away. Whatever he then said to the other women fighting for his attention caused them all to turn to her.

Having his absolute focus was exhilarating. Could she have that much sway with the man he'd dismiss five other women in favor of her? The guys he'd been talking to parted as she put her purse on the desk.

Connel leaned forward to snag her right wrist and tugged her into his lap. "Eleven fifty-nine," he murmured, sweeping her hair from her face. "You know how to follow an instruction to the letter."

She laughed, landing her smile on him. "Aye."

The side of his mouth tilted a fraction as it came toward hers. Everyone else faded to nothing, vanished from existence. His palm skimmed up the front of her thigh, squeezing her, possessing her, as the heat of his tongue sought hers. She'd thought he might be mad, that he might be upset. Why did it seem he was just happy to see her?

On an exhale, he turned his head, breaking the kiss. "Who's ready to play?" he called to the room.

Everyone cheered in response.

The grate of her zipper descending prompted her to grab the fabric at her chest and angle her chin to him. "I'm not wearing underwear."

He kissed her shoulder. "Can't get easier." His voice rose again. "Fuck off, all of you. Niall!"

Rising, Connel picked her up and dropped her on the narrow unit behind the desk, up against the backlit stag head emblem on the wall.

People filtered toward the curtain, the open curtain. Had she ever seen it pulled back like that? In spite of the guests slowing at the bottleneck, Connel unbuckled his belt as though they weren't even there.

Fuck, he turned her on.

"You hard for me, baby?" she asked, slipping off her shoes to slide the soles of her feet up the back of his legs.

"Aye," he grumbled.

"For me?" she asked. Damn it, damn the question. It wasn't meant to come out like that. Needy. Vulnerable. Weak. When his eyes rose to hers, it was clear he'd heard the doubt too. Shit, she'd meant to tease, not show distrust. Memories of his naked beauties apparently hadn't disappeared. "Sorry, I don't know why—"

"Shh," he said, cupping her jaw to raise her mouth higher. "How the fuck do you do this to me?"

Working on the buttons of his shirt, she gave in to the depth of his kiss. She hadn't even finished but spread her hands on his chest inside the fabric.

He broke the kiss, still cradling her face. "Missed that?"

Apparently, the thrill was no secret. "Feeling you with both hands? Yes." She laughed. "You have no idea."

His mouth sank onto hers again. The push and pull, gentle press, harder demand, it woke her need for him. Did it ever sleep? She couldn't believe it did. Even just thinking of him got her tingling in anticipation of the next time they'd be intimate.

As she opened his pants, it occurred to her she didn't know if they were alone. Shielded from the room by his body, she raised the embrace of her legs, pulling him closer.

"We need a rubber," she gasped her mouth from his, though he didn't give her the space to beg for long.

He surged forward, one hand leaving her face to descend between them until the head of his cock was right there at her threshold.

"Do we?" he panted, searching her eyes. "Your call, Macushla."

But it didn't need thought. Her head shook slightly, brushing her lips back and forth on his. The sweet solid girth of him forged forward inside her, slow, steady, his eyes assessing hers as a searing curl of pleasure coiled up through her gut.

Her eyes drifted shut. "Conn…" she breathed his name against his lips.

Catching the back of his neck, she moved, wriggling closer, arching and bowing, writhing against the delight she hadn't thought could get better. Damn, had she been wrong.

"Fuck," he hissed under his breath, his forehead landing on her head. "This was a mistake."

"Baby?" she asked, trying to stop moving, though it was near impossible. Her hand slid from the back of his neck around to his jaw, forcing him to lift his head to meet her eye. "Want to stop?"

"I couldn't pull out now if I had a damn cannon to my head."

Tipping her chin, she bounced higher, snagging his lower lip in her teeth.

As it slid free, she salved it with her tongue. "Fuck me, baby," she whispered, kissing his chin, his jaw, his throat. "Come in me. Inside me. Please."

Slowly, he withdrew only to surge in faster and pull out again, right to the cusp of her pussy, teasing her. His next harsh thrust wrung a yelp from her throat. The astute bastard knew what he was doing, exactly what he was doing. As proven when he took her hips and angled them, forcing her shoulders into the wall to hit her even deeper.

"Conn," she gasped as he sped up, slamming into her and sliding out, varying his pace as one arm hooked around the curve of her back.

Holding her there, he massaged her clit, accepting her clawing fingers and desperate cries as he forced her into the oblivion of orgasm. She called for him. Called for more. Begged for mercy. She didn't know what she wanted, what she needed. That didn't matter, he knew it.

"Conn! Conn!" she screamed.

He drove into her hard, yanking her body against his. Her muscles tensed, all of them, holding him in place as they reached their completion.

Something was… wrong. Different. What was…? Hard against him, him still inside her, there were blurs in her vision, prickling in her extremities. Her stomach was tight, her chest sore.

"Shit, Macushla," he breathed, his words as heavy as his exhales. His face was still in her hair; she couldn't see him. "You've never screamed for me like that… And I get you every time."

He did. With him, her needs were always met. Just like they'd started, he scooped up her face and married their mouths.

Was it the trust? Was it the lack of a barrier? That had been more intense. Hotter. More profound than anything they'd shared in the past.

"So this is doing business the Midwest McDades way?"

The female voice that interrupted their kiss startled her.

Connel twisted to look toward the door. "Doherty."

"McDade," the woman said.

He backed up to put himself away, giving her space to push down her dress and cover herself before he turned around.

She peeked by him expecting to see one woman. Instead, there were two, and a tall guy right behind them. Tall like Connel. Dark hair. The eyes...

"Oh my God," she whispered. "That's Razer McDade."

THIRTY-FOUR

"A REDHEAD," the shorter woman said. The stranger couldn't be more than an inch or two over five feet. "Is it natural?"

"Aye," Connel said as she slid off the unit to find her feet.

"Is she Catholic?"

"You don't give a shit," Razer said and shoved the other woman forward. "We have a problem."

Connel wasn't impressed. "I don't want her."

"No one does," the short woman said, folding her arms. "I still say we sell her."

"Who'd buy her?"

"Anyone interested in the bounty."

"A contract?" Connel asked. "Dead or alive?"

"Either," the woman said.

Connel flipped the lid off what she'd always thought was a cigar box and pulled out a gun to aim at the silent female.

Silent until the weapon came into view. Then she yelped and darted behind Razer.

The short woman grabbed Razer's arm to try yanking him aside, but he stayed put. "You said we couldn't collect," the petite beauty said. "Ire can."

"You didn't say you were bringing me here to die!" the woman behind Razer shrieked.

"My way would've been cleaner, husband," the brunette said.

Husband. She gasped and swerved around Connel. "You're Whisper Doherty!" Elation parted her lips. "Oh my God, you're gorgeous."

Whisper arched a brow and leaned back on her husband. "Is she hitting on me?"

"She's hot, I'd consider it," Razer said, curving an arm around his wife. "Could be a pro."

"Doesn't look like a pro," Whisper said. "Though she could be high class… maybe he pays more for the bruises… I don't need to pay for it."

"You don't."

"You would," Whisper said, reaching back to pat her husband's groin. "That thing should come with a license. The curse forced on all McDade wives and girlfriends. Am I right, High Class?"

The other woman squawked. "My life is in danger and you're joking about sex!" she said, marching around the couple to assert herself in front of them. "You're unbelievable."

"Never appreciative, are you, Pretty Nicki?" Whisper asked.

Another surge of excitement. "Are you Nicole McDade? You are!"

"Am I shooting Nic or not?" Connel asked.

"Yes," Whisper said in unison with Razer's…

"No."

Nicki seemed smug. "He won't murder me in front of his whore."

"Easy choice," Connel said, pulling back the

hammer.

Nicole yelped.

Sersha put a hand on his gun to lower it. "Why is there a contract on your head, Nicole?"

"Ask the who, not the why," Connel said. "I can make a call."

"We know who it is," Whisper said. "That's why we're here."

Niall came through the curtain that covered the back corner again. When he saw the group, he paused and said something in another language. Connel replied.

Whisper looked over her shoulder at her husband. "Why don't you speak Gaelic?"

"Why don't you?" he asked.

The lieutenant was polite enough to switch to English. "Want me to take the women next door?"

"What's next door?" Whisper asked, trying to push her husband back with her shoulders, but he didn't move.

"Party in the playroom."

"Oh!" Whisper exclaimed. "Sex party." She grabbed Razer's hand. "Sex party!"

"Cameras are on," Connel said.

"Doesn't matter," Whisper said. "You don't think there's footage of me and my husband screwing? Please, that shit's probably on YouTube."

"Peanut," Razer growled.

"Who cares about sex?" Nicole shrieked.

She flinched; the woman could be shrill.

"We got targets in that room?" Razer asked Connel behind her.

She didn't see his response. Was that why they'd had sex in the office? To avoid the cameras, or were they on in there too?

"Nothing we can't handle," Connel said. "Score on the move?"

"Yeah, Play's backing him up."

"Shy's keeping him sane," Whisper said. "By the way, you're welcome for that. If she and PJ weren't grounding him, he'd have laid waste to this whole damn city. Bosco's staying with them until we know what's going on. The Manzanis are coming for us?" She turned to her husband. "Think that's the Byrne's play?"

"While we're weak—"

"No one's weak," Connel said. "You've been out of the game too long. You wading back in, cousin?"

"No," Razer said, raising a hand.

Whisper caught it and wrapped his arm around her as she turned. "But we'll watch the shop if you need to travel."

"Why would I need to travel?"

"Madison Byrne."

A few beats went by.

"She comes to me," Connel said, "not the other way around."

"Okay, then call her. Get her here."

"I'm armed."

"Me too," Whisper said, folding her arms again.

Though in that dress, it didn't look like she had space for a weapon... maybe she meant her husband.

"Control your Doherty, cousin, or I'll do it for you."

"Give it a shot," Whisper said, taking a step. Razer caught her to pull her back. "You think I'm afraid of a fuck like—"

Razer closed a hand over her mouth, clamping her head against his torso. "You're disrespecting the man in his house," he grumbled against her. "Remember how we punish that?"

Whisper shoved his arm away while clenching her jaw. There were words in there, but she was fighting to restrain them.

Apparently surrendering, Whisper loosened. "Let's go downstairs and get drunk, High Class."

She didn't get far before Connel spoke. "High Class doesn't mix downstairs."

"It's that or the sex party," Whisper said, gesturing like she was weighing it for him.

Aware Connel wouldn't appreciate Whisper's defiance, she spun to face him and slipped her fingers through his.

"I can take them upstairs," she said. "If you want to talk business."

It took her laying a hand on his cheek to draw his focus down before he relaxed.

"Niall," he said, his eyes locked on hers as he issued foreign commands and put the gun back in its box. "We're leaving."

"Where are we going?" she asked, snatching her purse from the desk when he started across the room. "Home."

***

THE BENTLEY DOOR closed and they immediately started moving. Connel finished a call and hung up.

"Did you know they were coming?"

"No," he said, the growl in his expression betraying his anger. "The Doherty likes playing with fire."

Taking his hand from his thigh, she put it on hers, sliding it up under her skirt. His tension relaxed as he watched its progress.

Rather than speak, she reached for his face, guiding his mouth down to hers. "Calm, baby," she whispered as his lips trailed down her throat. "Conn…"

He laid her up against the side door, gathering her skirt up around her hips. "Why are we taking people back to our private space?" he asked, his hand sliding down her body from her throat to her cleavage and further south.

"Don't," she said, trying to close her thighs.

The frown he pinned on her was pissed, not just annoyed, offended. "What the fuck—"

"We don't have time to finish."

"We have the time I say we have," he said, caressing her legs. "Wanna go to a hotel?"

"My place is empty." When optimism lit his admiring eyes, she laughed. "But your family needs you."

He exhaled and sat up, hooking her legs over his lap as he did. "My family needs me to corral Madison Byrne. Her father put the bounty on Nicole's head."

"Your call?" He nodded, his palms skimming up and down her legs. "Why the bounty?"

"She insulted the family. That's the official line. Nicole insults a lot of people. There's something else behind this play." His hand stopped as his eyes closed and he pinched the bridge of his nose. "I could do without this bullshit."

"They're your family. Nothing is more important than family." She smiled when his eyes opened on her. "They came to you for help."

"There will be an ulterior motive."

"There always is," she said, her fingers curling around his on her thigh. "Why are they helping Nicole? Is she still a McDade?"

"Yes," he said.

"She's standing by Biz until he's released?"

"She can stand anywhere she wants, he won't have her. No self-respecting man would."

"Her? What did she do?"

He touched a loose tendril of hair by her temple. "Not all crimes were broadcast at the trial." He combed his fingers into her hair, cradling her head. "I'm neglecting you."

"No, you're not," she said. "Don't think that way. And if you want to drop me off at mine so you can deal with family stuff—"

"You're a McDade."

Gratitude only took them so far. "I know why you tell me that. You want to comfort me. To make me feel safe. And I appreciate that, I do…"

His hand descended. "But…?"

"I'm not a McDade, not really. Maybe I wanted to be, or I thought I could be, but… I'm the corrupted, not the corruptor."

"I'm the corruptor," he said, pushing her legs from his lap. "You're right, I have corrupted and exploited you. The council guys I'm paying off are at that party. I needed them to see you. To see us together so they'd relax about what comes next."

They'd talked about that before, so it wasn't a shock. No, that came in the icy detachment of his demeanor and snarling tone.

"Connel—"

"You've served your purpose, had your fun. We don't need to keep up the charade. Thanks for the tip on your father; I'll use that." When the car came to a stop, he buzzed down the privacy screen. "Don't get out. Just take her to her apartment."

He exited, slammed the door, and the car moved off.

That was… What was that? How had things changed so fast? Did he just break up with her… or had she broken up with him?

They'd neglected each other. The sex was great, but when it came to the talking, to opening up and sharing, they were no shining example.

Damnit. Double damnit. They needed to learn to communicate… if they got the chance.

THIRTY-FIVE

SHE COULDN'T SLEEP.

A couple of times, she'd been on the cusp of drifting off and then she'd remember. It happened so fast. How had it gone from what they'd shared in his office to him effectively dumping her on the curb?

Tossing back the covers, a glass of water would help. No, well, maybe a gallon of whiskey might knock her out, but she didn't feel like another trip to the hospital. If she started drinking, she may never stop.

Leaving the bedroom, she went around the breakfast bar to get a bottle of water from the fridge. Twisting off the cap, she was drinking as she turned to look into the room. The last thing she expected to see was Connel lying on her couch.

"Shit," she whispered, the water bottle descending to the breakfast bar.

How had he come in without her hearing him? And without a key. Though he had told her it was easy to pick locks.

Going over, she wasn't surprised to see his eyes

open. Yes, they were heavy, and his mood was definitely sour, but that could be for any number of reasons.

Opening her hand, she held it out to him. "Come to bed," she murmured.

When he was on his feet, she walked backwards, unbuttoning his shirt. His hands slid onto her waist, directing her around the furniture. As they crossed into the bedroom, she pushed his shirt from his shoulders and went to work loosening his fly. In unison with him shirking his pants, she wriggled out of her shorts, and he took her top off over her head.

When they were both naked, she finished backing up, sitting on the bed, sliding up it as he crawled on top of her.

She didn't even say anything as her legs parted and he continued between them, guiding himself into her as her body relaxed.

Satisfaction wrung a relieved sigh from her lips. Just being connected to him again was comfort. His support, his companionship, meant everything to her, more than she'd realized. His eyes stayed on hers as he moved within her. The barbs of need, the spikes of pleasure, it was cleansing. He cleansed her, kept her protected from every evil in the world.

He wanted to take care of her, but the truth was, that was impossible. What they had was immense, bigger than any other relationship she'd been a part of, romantic or otherwise. They had a connection, a way of talking without words, or conveying their intensity without ever uttering a syllable.

But that unique link was fragile. Not between them, but in relation to the rest of the world. How would they ever be together? Be more than what they were. There would always be naked women in his lap, kneeling at his feet. If she let herself slip too deep into him, she'd be hurt every time those other distractions showed themselves.

"Conn," she gasped in a whisper when climax consumed her.

The broad blanket of gratification soothed, even as he sped up to spend himself inside her.

He hadn't said a word. Didn't say a word even as he rolled to the side, taking her body with him to nestle her against him.

A tear slipped from her eye. The scorch of inevitability stole every illusion.

"Dorsey led the feds to their evidence," he said, his mouth in her hair. "Silvio wanted to kill her. They came to an understanding. So long as Hell is imprisoned, Dorsey is too."

"She was a child."

"Yeah, it was an innocent mistake," he said, his fingers combing her hair from her temple, back behind her ear, over and over. "The Manzanis keep her alive. She lives by their rules. We'll get her back… someday."

"What do they do to her?" she asked, relaxing her open hand on his chest. "Is she kept safe or do they… hurt her?"

"She lives better than Hell, by all accounts. She's kept in line. They've had her since she was four years old. They've indoctrinated her. She is what they want her to be. Completely compliant."

"That's why the cops stopped looking. Clancy told them to stop."

"Aye."

"He knows where she is… You didn't ever want to go get her?"

"The arrangement keeps the peace. We don't know exactly where she is, and they move her regularly. Finding out where, busting her out, it's risky."

"And why take the risk when you know she's safe?"

"Safer where she is than on the street."

"Especially after being locked up for so long," she said. "God knows what kind of contact she's had with the outside world. If any."

"We don't make waves. Don't reveal the arrangement and they keep her alive."

If she'd printed anything that even hinted at McDade cooperation with her investigation, Dorsey could've been killed in a second.

"I'm sorry," she said, turning her head just enough to rest her lips against him. "For your loss and for my interference."

"You didn't know," he said, still finger combing her hair. "Now you do…"

"I'll leave it alone. I already told Steeple I would."

"Without getting answers?"

"You said you'd tell me," she said. "I trusted you would."

He kissed her head. "Vex wants out from under his father. He believes Silvio's weak and wants to be more aggressive."

"Hence his Russian dolls," she said. "He's trying to build his own base."

"Aye, to ultimately challenge Silvio… or kill him."

"That's why he was in your office?"

"I give him cover for certain things, sponsor some of his operations, and we get a cut of the bigger pie… when there is one. He'll give us intel and sabotage his father's attempt to block the Harvest deal."

"So you and Evander are allies now."

She wasn't sure how to feel about that.

"As long as he's useful."

"You can't trust him," she said, aware Evander said the same thing about her. "I trust your gut, your instinct, but don't ever put your life in his hands. He'd sabotage even himself on impulse. If he has the chance to screw you over, he might take it. Even if it means screwing himself. Sometimes he just can't help himself."

"My guard's up." She kissed his chest. "But I am curious how this will play out. Doesn't hurt to have an intel source, or to be close to the epicenter at the time of detonation."

"Just protect yourself. Don't believe Evander, or any Manzani, will do it for you."

"I don't have final confirmation on your father's position," he said. "I'm doing as you asked and reserving judgement on his motivation. Babcock confirmed your grandfather has been asking questions and your father is around City Hall more than's required."

"If Silvio wants him to deliver votes or intel, he has to get close."

"I'm concerned he'll get desperate."

"Then what happens?" she asked, shifting the angle of her head. "I think what Silvio did to me proves he's close to desperate."

"Maybe."

"Maybe?"

"You didn't give them the information they wanted, but you got hurt. Very hurt. Sends a message to a guy."

"You think Silvio was sending you a message?"

"Or your father."

She loosened. "We wondered if Silvio had something on him. Maybe he's protecting the rest of us."

"Maybe."

Another maybe. It was so infuriating.

"I can call my grandfather. See if he has any reason to be worried. I'd ask Lach, but he'll want to know why I'm suddenly so interested in…" She was suddenly so interested because her father had revealed himself in the way he'd questioned her. By asking for information, he'd given her some useful intelligence in return. "Wow…"

Sitting up, she left his arms.

"Macushla?"

She didn't want to say the words but found his eyes and forced them out. "We're done, aren't we?"

"It's getting dangerous," he said. "The Byrnes, the Manzanis, even the Gambattos want to take us down. The McDades have to be bold. Assert our dominance. There could be payback."

One hit the other, so the other hit back. Where did it end?

"You're not afraid of that. Not afraid the other families will make a dent in what you've built. You've taken over every piece of Gambatto territory and then some. The other families come for you because you're powerful."

"Aye," he said, sitting up, shifting the pillows to lean against the headboard.

"So why now? It's been the same since we've been…" She couldn't say together because had they ever been? "Why come here if you were just going to dump me anyway?"

As her rage rose, she flipped around, but he seized her wrist to yank her back, forcing her body against his in an unyielding embrace.

"Being mine puts you in danger. More danger than being the superintendent's daughter, an alderman's granddaughter, any of it," he snarled. "You know how you survive being with a guy like me? Do you want to know what it will take?"

"What?" she huffed, struggling in his arms.

He clamped her tight, so tight her chest hurt. "Everything." Searching the ire in him, she needed more. "You do it by using me."

"I never wanted to use you," she argued, pissed

if he was going to accuse her of manipulating him with sex again.

"I can't protect you like this. I can't put word out that messing with you ends with looking down the barrel of my gun. If anyone came near you, tried to hurt or coerce you, the threat would end when you tell them I'll slit them open and rip out their guts just for breathing near you. To be with me, you have to be owned by me. Protected by me. You have to stand proud behind the McDade shield. You can't have one foot in their world and one in ours. When people try to hurt you, you tell them you're the superintendent's daughter."

"So?" she spat.

His face got closer. "The worst he'll do is arrest them." He startled her with a quick, brutish kiss. "Imagine how different that plays out when you tell the threat you belong to me." Her anger morphed into something much more intense, much more electrifying. "You wanted to know if I'd kill if you asked me to… Baby, you don't have to ask. Point and I'll shoot."

"If that's true…" she said, squeezing her arms up from where they were folded against him to coil them around his neck. "Why finish this? Whatever's between us—"

"Won't go away if we keep doing this."

His hold loosened. It didn't disappear, just diminished, yet she was bereft, terrified his arms would never hold her that way again.

"You've broken up with me before—"

"I'm not breaking up with you," he said. "This is us making this choice. The smart choice."

"To stay away from each other?"

"You were right in the car. If you're a McDade, you're all in. You all in, baby? No secrets. No lies. You ready to tell the world you're mine? That I'm your McDade?"

Now it made sense. Putting it in words, telling him she wasn't really a McDade got him thinking, facing the truth.

"You're dangerous," she murmured.

"That danger will get you killed if you don't let me protect you."

What future could they have? Happiness? Marriage? Kids? Yeah, right. Connel sitting down to Thanksgiving dinner with Lachlan and Whisper Doherty?

All that would start with her telling her family. Telling her dad. Her grandfather. And if her dad was in deep with Manzani and her relationship with Connel came out… They'd all be in danger.

"You know the man I am," he said, running his fingers into her hair.

"And I was never ashamed of that," she said. "The things you've done for me—"

"I'll always do those things for you."

"But you won't be in my bed," she said, sinking away from him on her knees to sit on her feet. "Every day I'll wake up lonely."

"If I got my way, you would," he said, provoking her frown. "The thought of any other guy in my place…"

As his jaw worked, his anger grew palpable.

Lying on her side, she laid her head in his lap. "How do you think I felt tonight…?" She traced a fingertip down the ridges of his abs. "Why does your family need your help with Madison Byrne?"

"Because she and her father are close," he said and inhaled. "And because keeping them in line involves me, her, and a hotel room."

That was what she'd suspected. "Right."

When she tried to rise, he laid a hand on her temple to keep her down. "Cushla Machree—"

"I know, we're through, and we were never

exclusive. We weren't…"

"That why we stopped using rubbers?" he asked and their eyes met. "No one else is here tonight, Macushla."

Her favorite time with him. Alone. In the dark. In the night.

"I love it when you call me that," she said. "I don't know what it means, but it sounds poetic, romantic. What do I call you in return?"

"To you I'm…" He thought about it for a second before meeting her eye again, stroking the hair by her temple. "Do rún."

"You're do rún?" she asked, trying to copy the accent. He kept caressing but gave a single nod. "I didn't know the language was so sexy." She sighed. "I'd love to just lie here and listen to your words all night. Your accent melts me all the way through. And you're going to take it, take the way you make me feel, away forever."

"Tonight is ours," he said.

"Evander will come looking for me tomorrow."

"And I'll tell him we both lost you."

Rising, she straddled him, taking hold of the headboard behind him to support her weight. "I'll always be in your corner too… No one can take what only we know."

THIRTY-SIX

LYING ON THE COUCH, some infomercial was playing on the TV as she typed on the laptop balanced on her stomach.

The first sound stopped her typing. There was a click, a snap and…

Grabbing up the laptop, she put it on the floor as she flipped over to watch the front door over the edge of the arm of the couch.

Damn, she needed a gun, should have got a gun from somewhere.

The door swung open. As soon as she registered her brother, she exhaled.

"What the hell?" she exclaimed, throwing off her blanket to leap up. "What do you think you're doing?"

"Oh, good, you are alive," Lachlan said, tucking something into his pocket.

His lock pick doohickey, no doubt.

"I'm calling the cops," she said, snatching her phone from the end table.

He opened his arms. "At your service."

"You know you swore to serve and protect," she said, shaking her phone at him. "How is breaking into an innocent woman's apartment protection?"

He sauntered to her fridge. "If you answered your phone, I wouldn't have to break in," he said, sniffing a box of three- or four-day-old Chinese food. His face contorted in disgust. "Shit, looks like I showed up just in time."

"You didn't show up just in time. You shouldn't have shown up at all."

He swung the fridge door closed to wander over. "You do remember, like, two weeks ago being attacked and hospitalized?"

"Yes, I do, but—"

"And I told you I was worried about you, asked you to stay at mine." He stopped in front of her, a frown forming as he surveyed the living room before finally zeroing in on her. "Who was he?"

"Who was who?"

"The only time you live on take out and work on the couch with the TV playing bullshit is if you've had your heart broken."

"You don't know what you're talking about."

"It's Wednesday, you get that? Steeple hasn't seen you since last week. If this is the trauma catching up to you—"

"This is nothing catching up to me. In fact, I ordered a 'Dealing with Trauma' audio package already."

"It's not working."

"These things take time," she said, watching him go around her to step over the laptop and sit down. "I didn't invite you to stay."

"This couch pulls out, right?" he asked and bounced on it.

"Why do you care?"

"Because I'm staying," he said, laying his arms along the back.

"No, you're not," she said, rushing over to stand in front of him.

While she was heating up, he seemed so relaxed, which didn't help his case much.

"You're my sister. It's my job to look out for you."

"I don't want to be your job—"

"I want to look out for you," he said, narrowing his eyes. "You didn't stop McDade doing it. Why would you have a problem with me doing the same thing?"

"Maybe because you're my brother."

"Hiding something?"

"Is that what this is? You're investigating me?"

"I want you to be safe. I don't want to spend days worrying about you because you don't pick up your phone. I gave you the chance to do this your way—"

"You can't move into my apartment."

"Because? Why would you worry about me investigating you unless there was something to find? How many guys are you dating?"

Zero. Which was kind of the problem.

"That's none of your business," was what came out. "I could be screwing twenty guys. If I was, having my brother around might put a dampener on my social life."

"If you were, someone would be home checking up on you." He smacked the couch cushion next to him. "Sit down, sister. This is happening whether you like it or not."

TO BE CONTINUED...

Thank you for reading this tale!
If you can, please take the time to review.

~

Ask your local library for more Scarlett Finn novels!

~

For all things Scarlett Finn
check out:

www.scarlettfinn.com

BOOK THREE

SCARLETT FINN

OUT NOW!